D0041570

TORCHWOOD

SKYPOINT

The *Torchwood* series from BBC Books:

1. ANOTHER LIFE
   Peter Anghelides

2. BORDER PRINCES
   Dan Abnett

3. SLOW DECAY
   Andy Lane

4. SOMETHING IN THE WATER
   Trevor Baxendale

5. TRACE MEMORY
   David Llewellyn

6. THE TWILIGHT STREETS
   Gary Russell

7. PACK ANIMALS
   Peter Anghelides

8. SKYPOINT
   Phil Ford

9. ALMOST PERFECT
   James Goss

TORCHWOOD
SKYPOINT

Phil Ford

2 4 6 8 10 9 7 5 3 1

Published in 2008 by BBC Books, an imprint of Ebury Publishing
A Random House Group company

Torchwood is a BBC Wales production for BBC Television
Executive Producers: Russell T Davies and Julie Gardner

Original series created by Russell T Davies and broadcast on BBC Television

The Random House Group Limited Reg. No. 954009.
Addresses for companies within the Random House Group can be found at www.randomhouse.co.uk.

A CIP catalogue record for this book is available from the British Library.

ISBN 978 1 846 07575 9

The Random House Group Limited supports The Forest Stewardship Council (FSC), the leading international forest certification organisation. All our titles that are printed on Greenpeace approved FSC certified paper carry the FSC logo. Our paper procurement policy can be found at www.rbooks.co.uk/environment

Commissioning Editor: Albert DePetrillo
Series Editor: Steve Tribe
Production Controller: Phil Spencer

Cover design by Lee Binding @ Tea Lady © BBC 2008
Typeset in Albertina and Century Gothic
Printed in Great Britain by Clays Ltd, St Ives plc

Dedicated to Hayley

ONE

Gwen Williams.

That was going to take some getting used to.

It had been a little over two weeks now. They had been away. Ten days in Cuba. It was the rainy season, and it had rained every day, but not one drop had mattered. And she had been Gwen Williams all that time, but holidays – especially honeymoons – are not the real world. It was like a game out there.

But now she was back.

Cardiff, the real world. Or what passed for it these days.

Mrs Williams.

Whoa! Some things you got used to, like living on a rift in time and space, aliens stalking the sewers that would tear your throat out as easily as look at you, others that got you pregnant on your hen night with a bite…

But some things she thought she'd just never get used to.

The estate agent had called her 'Mrs Williams' when he

met them in the lobby.

Mr and Mrs Williams.

It felt strange, but nice.

But twenty minutes later, when that same estate agent vanished into thin air, that was something Gwen Williams née Cooper felt more than qualified to handle.

TWO

Rhys was glowing as she came through the door. He was standing behind the kitchen counter wearing a smile so wide he could've been modelling for a Warner Brothers cartoon. It had been their first day back at work, and the smile could have just been that newlywed joy of seeing her again after their first ten hours apart since the wedding ceremony. On the other hand, Rhys and Gwen might have shared the same name for only about a fortnight, but they had shared this one-bedroom flat and a lot more besides for the last four years. This wasn't just Rhys's glad-to-see-you smile, this was his I-can't-wait-to-tell-you full beam.

'Good day?' he asked.

'Not bad. Bit of a Weevil hunt out Splott-way, but it was just the one and it had a limp.'

The first time she had come across one of the sewer-dwelling aliens had been in a corridor of the Royal Cardiff Infirmary. She had thought it was some guy in a Halloween mask complete with five-centimetre fangs. It had then proceeded to use them to all but take the head off some poor bastard that had got in its way. But back then – little more than a year ago – she had just been a green police constable. These days the most remarkable thing about a Weevil was that *this one had a limp*? Yes, welcome back to the real world. Welcome back to Cardiff.

Then Rhys was kissing Gwen. And whatever it was that he was burning to tell her, he had also missed her.

'At least you're home on time. That's a good start.'

'I told Jack I had to get back to make sure I had my old man's tea on,' she joked.

Rhys didn't notice. His excitement was taking over.

'Never mind tea. We'll eat out afterwards.'

'After what?'

But Rhys was already grabbing his coat. 'We'll go to one of the restaurants on the Bay. It won't be far.'

'Far from where?'

'You'll see. We've got an appointment at half-six.'

Gwen shook her head and followed him out through the door. Rhys loved delivering surprises. It was one of the things she loved about him. The biggest surprise of all had been how he had put up with everything she had brought to their relationship since she'd seen that Weevil in the hospital corridor and run into Jack Harkness for the first time. And that was why she loved Rhys most of all. Because he loved her, would do anything for her, and accepted so much that no other man ever could.

Rhys didn't put his life on the line every day to save the world from savage alien creatures washed onto Cardiff's inter-dimensional shoreline by a rift in time and space. He managed trucks and drivers for Harwood's Haulage. Oh, he knew about the aliens – he'd run into one or two in recent months – but he left the Men in Black routine to Jack, Owen, Toshiko, Ianto – and, of course, Gwen herself. They were Torchwood. Nevertheless, it was Rhys that was her hero.

All the same, when he was pulling up in the car park of a steel-and-glass apartment building fifteen minutes later, Gwen thought that her hero had finally cracked under the pressure.

'You are joking,' she said.

The sun was setting across the Bay, a sinking ball of fire that burned like napalm on the flat water and turned the dimmed glass panels of the apartment building into planes of molten Aztec gold.

The hoarding alongside the apartment building called it SkyPoint. *An exclusive development of two- and three-bedroom apartments for state-of-the-art living.*

Gwen wondered what on Earth constituted state-of-the-art living.

If you're going to be anyone in Cardiff, you're going to be at SkyPoint!

And that might be true, but she wondered how the hell Rhys thought they could possibly afford to be one of them.

But Rhys was already out of the car, looking up at the building.

'Just look at it, Gwen. Isn't it beautiful?'

Over the last ten years, the face of Cardiff had changed so much that, if it had been a kid, its own mother would have passed it by on the street without a second glance. If you took a look out of any high-rise window across the city, you would see almost as many cranes hanging over the place as you would skyscrapers shouldering for prominence. But Gwen had never considered any of the lean sun-flaring steel and glass giants *beautiful*. Impressive, for sure. Dynamic, no doubt. Welcome, too – Gwen could just remember the drab, emasculated town that had been left by the closure of the valley mines, and the loss of the docks that had distributed that black Welsh gold around the world. When the docks had gone, what had been left had been a bitter and dark spectre of what Cardiff had once been. But that now lay buried beneath these shiny new buildings and Cardiff's spirit had been resurrected. It was once again a boom town. Perhaps that did make SkyPoint beautiful.

On the other hand, Rhys was the kind of bloke that applied the word to a blood-red six-wheel Freightliner tractor unit kitted out with so much dazzling chrome it had to be a danger to other road users.

'There's no way we can afford this, Rhys,' she said. But she said it with a smile, not wanting to puncture his enthusiasm, not wanting to spoil their first proper week as newlyweds with an argument over money.

'I'm not talking about the penthouse, love. Just a little two-bedroom apartment. Sixth floor. Doesn't even have to have a Bay view.'

'I like where we live now. What's wrong with it?'

'Nothing's wrong with it. Except that was the old you and me. PM. Pre-Marriage. This is us AM—'

'After Marriage. Yes I get it, Rhys. I still don't see the point.'

'It's like a statement, isn't it? Moving on. We're going forward.' Then he looked at her, held her hands. 'Two bedrooms.'

Gwen raised an eyebrow and kinked one corner of her mouth. 'You're not talking about when you snore and I kick you out of bed, are you?'

Rhys said nothing, just raised his eyebrows a fraction, and returned her smile.

They were talking in eyebrow semaphore, and they'd only tied the knot two weeks ago. God, they were like an old married couple already. Maybe Rhys was right – they needed a new start.

'Come on, then,' she said, tugging him towards the building's glass doors. 'But we're just looking. Maybe get some decorating ideas for our place.'

'Whatever you say,' he smiled.

Glass doors the colour of bonfire smoke parted before them, and they stepped into a large reception area that Gwen was surprised to find quite comfortable. She had expected to find more cold steel and glass, somewhere as sterile as Owen's Autopsy Room back at the Hub. But the SkyPoint reception was furnished with white, greys and blacks that were at once modern and comforting. They crossed a short-pile carpet that muffled their steps and Rhys gave their name to a blonde girl in a short black skirt who sat at a low table in one corner of the reception area decorated with a sweep of colour brochures.

'Mr and Mrs Williams,' he said. 'We've got an appointment with Mr Shaw.'

The blonde girl in the short black dress uncurled her legs

and smiled at Rhys, and Gwen felt a pang of something. Not so much jealousy as proprietorial supremacy.

Rhys is all mine, love, signed and sealed, so you might as well put those legs away, for all the good they'll do you.

The blonde whispered into the phone that sat alongside the brochures, and Rhys gave Gwen a smile as he took in the reception. Gwen noted with delight that Rhys barely looked at the girl's legs. Was that marriage for you, or just excitement over the apartment they were going to see? A part of her wanted to tell him again that, whatever this Mr Shaw showed them, there was no way they could afford it. She had never been entirely sure who it was that signed the Torchwood pay cheques – the money just appeared in her bank account on the first of every month – but, whoever they were, the wages bore no comparison to the dangers involved in their earning. As a general rule, if you wanted to make a fortune it seemed you had to come up with another way of ending the world, not saving it.

An elevator door opened as the blonde girl put down her phone. The man that stepped out of it wasn't the estate agent, although, immaculately groomed and dressed in black Armani, he could have been. Gwen had never laid eyes on Mr Shaw and she had never met the good-looking, lean man that stepped from the elevator – but she had seen him before. She never forgot a police file.

And there were a lot of files on Besnik Lucca. No convictions, but a whole heap of paperwork that went nowhere.

Lucca caught Gwen's eye. He wouldn't know her. Wouldn't know that she used to be a cop. But there was something in that glance that made Gwen's stomach churn. Lucca was in his early forties, the slightest threads of grey in his thick, black hair. He was tanned, worked out and moved like a man who owned the space he moved through. He looked nothing like a Weevil. But he had the same look in his dark eyes. He was a predator.

Lucca switched his glance from Gwen to the blonde girl, whose eyes were already ripping the Armani from his shoulders and tearing apart the crisp white linen beneath.

He smiled at her. He didn't need to say anything.

The girl shivered with excitement, the way she might had his fingers teased her flesh with a sliver of ice. 'Good evening, Mr Lucca.'

Lucca backed up his magnesium-flare smile with a wink, and the girl's skin prickled with secret goose bumps as the man in black slid out of the building.

Gwen thought she had only met one other man that could have that kind of an effect on women, and other men. And she knew there were dark places within Jack Harkness, but they were nothing to the black pit of Besnik Lucca's soul.

She watched the smoked-glass doors close behind Lucca and turned to the blonde. 'Excuse me. Does that man live here?' she asked.

The girl smiled back, thinking she knew exactly what Gwen was thinking. She couldn't have been more wrong. 'Mr Lucca has the penthouse,' she said.

Gwen grabbed Rhys's arm and started dragging him towards the door.

'I'm sorry, Rhys. No way can we live here.'

Rhys pulled himself free.

'What are you talking about? Why?'

'That man. I know him.'

'The guy in the Armani?' And then a light went on in Rhys's head. 'Oh no – don't tell me. He's an alien. Right?'

Gwen glanced back at the blonde girl. They were halfway between her table and the sliding glass door, and she was watching them with a distracted curiosity, or perhaps she was hoping Lucca had forgotten his mobile or car keys or something and would sweep back in again. Either way, Gwen just hoped she hadn't heard the A-word.

'No, he's not,' she said, and tried to make it as forceful as she could, considering it was a whisper. 'But he is a crook. And not just any crook, probably the biggest, most dangerous, bastard of a crook in Cardiff – if not Wales.'

Rhys looked at her, took it all in, and said, 'So?'

'*So*? What the hell do you mean, *so*?'

'Gwen, you're not a police officer any more. What does it matter what the bloke in the penthouse does for a living? Do you know what that guy on the floor below us now does?'

'I know he isn't Besnik Lucca. When I was on the force we had a file on him so big they needed a fork-lift to move it around. Robbery, extortion, prostitution, pornography, *murder*, Rhys. We were investigating him for every crime in the book.'

'*Investigating*. So none of it was ever proven?'

'Who the hell are you, his lawyer?'

'What does it matter, Gwen? So he lives on the top floor of the block. I promise I won't invite him to the house-warming.'

'Rhys, the man is a killer.'

'Gwen, there are killers in the sewers. They don't stop me taking a crap when I need one.'

Gwen stopped dead, somehow felt a carpet being ripped from beneath her. She wanted to tell him that this was different. Instead she felt one corner of her mouth trying to curl into a smile. God, she hated it when Rhys made her smile when she didn't want to.

And that was when the elevator doors opened again, and the estate agent walked out towards them, one hand springing out ahead of him, intent on some serious welcome-pumping.

'Mr and Mrs Williams. I'm Brian Shaw. Welcome to SkyPoint.'

Rhys took Shaw's hand and shook it, but his eyes were on Gwen.

Oh what the hell? We're only looking, aren't we?

And Gwen shook his offered hand, and smiled, pushing her worries about Lucca to the back of her mind. Sod it, she was just going to enjoy the tour. If anyone was going to burst Rhys's bubble, less than a month into their marriage, it would be the bank manager.

Shaw led them across the reception area and into the waiting mirror-panelled elevator. He was maybe thirty-five, with sandy, swept-back hair that had started to thin at the front. He wore a dark suit over a white shirt that gleamed like a soap-powder ad, and a tie sprinkled with tiny clowns. When Gwen caught a glimpse of his cufflinks there were clowns there, too. It looked like the sort of birthday combo a girlfriend might buy her fella if he had a quirky thing about guys with red noses and baggy trousers. Brian Shaw may have been an estate agent, but maybe he was a nice guy, after all, she thought.

The elevator took them up to the tenth floor and the doors slid open with a *ping* that was so discreet, it could have been the sound of a pin dropping. Smiling, Brian Shaw led them out into a passageway lit with frosted-glass uplighters.

'There are twenty-five floors. A hundred and twenty-five apartments in all,' Shaw explained as he led them along the passageway to a black door. 'Two-bedroom and three-bedroom, all en suite.' The door was marked *thirty-two* in small unobtrusive brushed steel lettering. There were no digits on the doors, Gwen noticed; figures were maybe too gauche for SkyPoint's understated residents.

'Fully equipped kitchens, appointed to the highest standard,' Shaw continued as he unlocked the door with an electronic key. 'And as you see, security here is both discreet and practically unbreachable.' And that was a comfort with a man on the top floor who, according to one story, deep-fried a man's bollocks while he was still attached to them. 'I think you're going to be quite impressed,' said the estate agent, and he led them into the apartment.

Rhys stepped aside with a smile and motioned for Gwen to go first. And there really was no way she could argue with Brian Shaw – she was definitely impressed. The door led directly into a massive open-plan lounge-kitchen-diner (whatever the proper estate agent speak was for that), but it wasn't the room that took her breath away – it was the Bay that lay beyond it.

The sun was now little more than a golden crest on the horizon, the sky had turned a deep, rich scarlet, and the water sparkled beneath it like a mirror scattered with jewels. Around it, the waterside development of the city gathered, cast in partial silhouette by the evening light, like an audience for the setting sun.

She felt Rhys beside her. 'What do you think?' he asked.

She wanted to tell him that the spectacle made no difference – there was no way they were moving. Instead she breathed, 'It's beautiful.'

Behind them, Brian Shaw grinned. 'And that's only the view. Wait till you take a look around the apartment.'

'Yeah, right, mate,' said Rhys, eager as a kid with a sled on a snow-swept Saturday. 'Show us everything.'

And Brian Shaw went into demonstrator mode. The lounge – which would easily accommodate the entirety of Gwen's old flat – was ready-wired with a wall-mounted TV screen that doubled as a mirror and looked like you could organise a drive-in picture show around it. When Brian fired it up, the Hi-Def picture blazed, and the sound boomed from hidden speakers all around the room. Rhys made a note: the beach landing in *Saving Private Ryan* was going to be mega on this baby. The speakers were also hooked into a sound system that emerged from the wall at the touch of a remote-control button (and the same remote operated the TV, the powered window blinds, the dimming lights, and probably the toilet flush, for all Rhys knew).

The kitchen was no less high-tech and stylish, all black granite and chrome with halogen lights over the work surfaces that somehow knew where you were and intensified intelligently to light your chopping, mixing, or whatever else you got up to on the kitchen counters. (And sometimes Rhys and Gwen got up to stuff that wasn't strictly speaking culinary.) The fridge was connected to the internet and could order the groceries for you, the eco-friendly washing machine measured the water it used and fed itself with detergent. The dishwasher did everything but load itself.

You got used to high-tech gear when you worked for Torchwood – it had spent a century scavenging alien technology and developing it for its own needs – but Gwen's idea of a cutting-edge kitchen gadget was a shopping-channel gizmo for dicing onions. She wondered if Jack had maybe got some backdoor deal with a kitchenware developer manufacturing alien food-blending technology.

Then the estate agent led them through into the master bedroom. In the room they shared at the moment there was just about enough space for a double bed and one wardrobe with a rail that sagged with clothes. Gwen had a small dressing table, but she had to sit on the side of the bed to use it as there was no room for a stool. But here the superking bed was the width of a Cadillac and there was space to park another one either side. There wasn't a wardrobe – there was a dressing room.

'Didn't you say you always wanted a dressing room?' Rhys grinned.

Gwen gave him a look. Yes, she'd always wanted a dressing room and this place was fantastic – but, *come on!* There was still no way they could afford to live here. Unless maybe she started selling alien tech to the blender people.

Meanwhile, Brian Shaw was on the move again, sliding back a dark, frosted-glass door. 'Through here we have the en suite wetroom, furnished in grey slate and black granite.'

The estate agent walked into the bathroom, and Gwen caught Rhys's sleeve as he went to follow him.

'This is madness, Rhys,' she whispered. 'It's beautiful, yes, I know. But we just can't afford any of this. We're just wasting this man's time.'

Rhys looked into her eyes, touched her cheek. 'I know,' he said softly. 'Maybe not now. But one day. Soon. You and me, this is what we want, isn't it? The best we can get.'

Gwen smiled at him and squeezed his hand. 'I've already got that.'

He winked at her. 'Come on. Let's go see the granite lavvy.'

Gwen burst out laughing and Rhys led her through the frosted-glass door.

They took it in. It was – as the estate agent had said – all grey slate and black granite, with stark white fittings and chrome taps.

But there was no sign of Brian Shaw.

Rhys glanced back over his shoulder, like there was any chance at all of Shaw having slipped past him unseen. 'Where did he go?'

The logical mechanics of Gwen's mind, the cerebral technology that refused to give in despite all that she had seen after the last year or so, shifted a gear. 'He must have come out when we were talking.'

And she was already out of the wetroom, calling out for the estate agent. 'Mr Shaw?'

But there was no answering call.

Gwen swept through the flat quickly. The apartment was big, but it wasn't that big. And Brian Shaw wasn't in it.

She found Rhys still in the wetroom. She wasn't sure if he was really considering the possibility that Brian Shaw had vanished down the plughole.

'He's not here,' she said.

'He must be somewhere. He walked in here not twenty seconds ahead of us. There's no window.'

Her logic-gearing did another shift. Given that this was Cardiff, and that Cardiff was built on a tear in time and space that sometimes warped what most people took for reality, sometimes the logical explanation for the inexplicable came down to two words…

'The Rift,' she said.

Rhys looked at her, shook his head. 'Oh, no. Not here?'

'So you explain it to me, Rhys. You tell me how Brian Shaw walked into the bathroom and disappeared without so much as a flush.'

He couldn't.

She kissed him gently.

'What was that for?'

'I'm sorry, Rhys. I'm going to have to go back to work.'

THREE

Toshiko Sato loved equations the way that other people loved poetry.

Those people, the poetry lovers – the people that most others probably thought of as *normal* – found truth and emotional support in the structure of words, the rhythm and the cadence of their sounds. Toshiko had never fully trusted words. They were so easy to misinterpret, or to be misused. A lot of people could be very clever with words. And they used them to break your heart. Not so many were quite that clever with numbers, few really understood them beyond their significance on a bank statement, and fewer still appreciated their simple, truthful beauty in the way that Toshiko Sato did. Because, at the end of the day, everything came down to numbers, from the physics of an atomic bomb to the shape of an autumn leaf swept away on the wind. Everything came down to mathematics. It was that kind of vision that made Toshiko special. It was also, she knew, what made her a freak.

The fact that she was in love with a dead man who wouldn't quit walking and talking was par for the course.

Superfreak!

She looked up from the figures on her computer screen – calculations on Rift energy fluctuations – and watched Owen bound up the steel staircase to tend his collection of alien plants. He didn't move badly for a man who had had his heart smashed to a pulp by a .44 calibre bullet just a couple of months earlier. He still had the hole in his chest; like the finger that he had purposefully broken before her one night in a vicious black mood, it would never heal. One morning, he had turned up in the Hub with flowers poking out of the wound and told everyone he thought Torchwood's subterranean base needed cheering up. Being dead hadn't killed Owen's sense of humour. Or perhaps, like her numbers, it was just a way to cope.

Toshiko had been in love with Owen Harper for two years, since he had joined Torchwood. Then he had been a man scarred by the loss of his fiancée to an alien brain parasite who had tried to lose himself in booze and a nightly succession of anonymous club-shags. But a part of her believed that she had come to love him even more since the bullet from that automatic had ripped his chest apart.

Superfreak!

And the big circular airlock door rolled aside. And Toshiko was grateful for the interruption to her thoughts.

Gwen was back.

'I thought you'd gone home,' Toshiko called.

Gwen was unique within Torchwood – she had a home and a life to go to. Which was why Toshiko and Owen were still at the Hub. And Jack and Ianto were still around, somewhere, doing something – albeit probably more recreational.

Gwen was closing on Toshiko, urgent. 'I need you to look for Rift activity in the Bay area.'

Owen stuck his head over the railings above, a faintly luminous blue-green plant in one hand, and a small plastic watering can in the other. 'Something cracking off?' he asked.

'I don't know. Maybe.'

Gwen got Toshiko to check the coordinates for the SkyPoint location. She drew a blank.

'Nothing,' Toshiko said. 'No records of Rift activity. Nothing at all.'

Gwen frowned.

'Hey, watch that. You'll get lines.'

The voice sounded American. Whether or not Jack Harkness was American was something else. They all knew that wasn't his name. The real Jack Harkness had died in an aeroplane over England in 1941. Their Jack – this Jack – had never felt any compulsion to tell them his real name; he said it didn't matter. The man that went by the name he once used belonged to another time, and no longer existed.

The mysteries that surrounded Jack Harkness were impenetrable but, as they had come to learn, unimportant. What mattered was that Jack – wherever he was from, whoever he really was – would always be there for them.

Until he disappeared again. And even then, he would be back.

But Jack wasn't going anywhere right now. He wanted

to know what had broken Gwen away from her new husband so quickly and brought her back to the Hub. He was buttoning the last couple of buttons on his blue service shirt as he asked and, as Gwen quickly ran through events at SkyPoint, she saw Ianto Jones appear. He was as discreet as the tailored suit on his back, and the only hint of any connection between Jack's buttons and Ianto Jones was the latter's momentary adjustment of his tie as he glanced into the reflective surface of an inactive monitor.

Jack heard Gwen out without a word, then raised an eyebrow. 'Just vanished?'

'All but in front of my eyes,' Gwen confirmed.

'But according to my instruments, there's no indication of Rift activity in that area,' Toshiko said.

'But estate agents don't just vanish into thin air,' Ianto observed. 'We're just not that lucky.'

Owen was sitting on the steel steps that led to his alien hydroponics. 'But if there's no sign of Rift activity…?'

'I know,' Jack smiled. 'Intriguing, isn't it?' He glanced at his watch, then at Toshiko. 'You want to go flat-hunting?'

'I'll get my gear,' she said.

And Ianto was already holding Jack's old RAF greatcoat for him as he shrugged it on.

'I'm coming, too,' said Gwen.

But Jack shook his head. 'No you're not. First day back to work after your honeymoon? You're going back home to Rhys, cook him dinner or go buy fish and chips. Watch TV. Make-believe life is ordinary just once more. For his sake.'

Gwen thought about arguing, and then thought about Rhys. Life was never going to be ordinary, but Jack was right, she owed it to Rhys to pretend it was. If only tonight.

'You ready?' Jack asked Toshiko as she pulled a messenger bag of Rift and alien-hunting tech in place over her shoulder.

'Ready.'

'It's apartment thirty-two,' Gwen called after Jack and Toshiko as they headed towards the airlock. 'Tenth floor.'

'Thirty-two. Tenth floor,' Jack called back without looking, and the huge circular door rolled back into place.

It was only then that she wondered whether she should have mentioned the border-line psychopath that lived on the top floor. But she decided that Jack had handled worse things than Besnik Lucca.

FOUR

The crisp white linen shirt that Besnik Lucca had been wearing earlier that evening when he had left SkyPoint was no longer white.

No amount of laundering was going to fix it.

Arterial blood didn't come out. He supposed that was in the nature of it. Arterial blood wasn't supposed to come out. But the edge of a razor blade sliced across each thigh of a double-crossing kid hung upside down like a pig on a hook will bring it out, all right. Especially on the first cut, when the blood pressure is still high. That was the gush that had caught him on the chest – and Lucca hadn't been the one doing the cutting. Lucca had a man who was good with blades to slice flesh for him. It was he who appreciated that hanging a man upside down before you cut the femoral artery meant that death took that much longer. And Lucca appreciated that kind of expertise, especially when it came to dealing with low-life scum at the bottom end of his organisation who entertained dreams of ripping off their boss. The exsanguinated eighteen-year-old's corpse would serve as a reminder to those other foot soldiers of their position in life. It was worth one spoiled shirt. Lucca was only thankful that he had removed his Armani jacket to personally soften the kid up a little before the blade man had practised his craft.

Lucca left the kid strung up, sobbing and dying, and wishing to God that he had never even thought of cutting flour into his boss's coke and cutting him out of the extra profit. As he left, despite the ruined shirt, Lucca was smiling.

Fifteen minutes later, Lucca had crossed the city and was sliding his black Porsche into the underground parking bay reserved for him beneath SkyPoint. He had listened to Wagner as he drove. Lucca loved Wagner and, almost 200 years apart, they had both had their reasons for going under the wire to escape Latvia so he felt they shared a kindredship.

The parking bay was alongside the apartment block's service elevator that would take Lucca directly to his floor. No one would see the blood on his shirt. It was the very reason he had specified this parking bay as his own when he put money into the SkyPoint project.

By the time he had tapped the entrance code into the security keypad and stepped into the elevator, he had forgotten the name of the kid he had left bleeding to death on the other side of town.

As the heavy steel doors of the service elevator closed on Lucca, the only witness to his arrival was a hidden security camera, but that didn't worry him. The only place those pictures were going was a panel of monitors in his own apartment. Besnik Lucca was forty-two years old, and he planned to see at least as many years again – and he knew the only way to do that was to be tough, and to be careful. And that was why he had invested so much money into SkyPoint: it wasn't just an apartment block rising like any other on Cardiff's crowded skyline – it was Besnik Lucca's fortress.

Lucca left the elevator on the twenty-fifth floor and keyed another code into another security pad, then pushed the door open into his penthouse. Lights automatically activated as he stepped across the threshold. That meant that no one had been moving around in there, and that meant that Carmen was still on the bed where he had left her. There was no chance that she had dressed and gone out; he hadn't given her the code that would allow her through the door. She didn't go anywhere unless he said so. And in the two weeks since he had brought her back to the apartment, the thought of going anywhere had never seemed to cross her mind. But heroin was like that. You could get a taste for it pretty fast.

He didn't bother to look in on the girl. He walked straight past her door and into his own bedroom. The city and the Bay lay at his feet, dark now but sparkling with the lights of bars and restaurants, and other apartments. He stripped off and enjoyed the reflected image of himself, a naked god astride the city below, then stepped into the shower and purged himself of the stink of the young drug dealer's death.

There was a TV screen built into the marble of the shower

wall and a waterproof remote hung alongside the soaps and lotions Lucca kept beside the shower controls. He used it as the shower water beat down on him like a warm tropical storm, and the screen lit up with footage from the SkyPoint lobby.

A time code at the bottom of the screen told him he was watching something from mid-afternoon when nothing was really happening down there, apart from the blonde girl from the estate agency admiring her reflection in one of the smoked windows. He smiled as she adjusted her neckline for a fraction more exposure. The girl had no idea about Lucca's hidden surveillance network. No one but Lucca and the people who had installed it did. If anyone ever came to get him – some other company intent on his turf, or someone from the old country that was still looking for his head; maybe even the cops – then Lucca would see them coming, and he'd be ready. And he was prepared, even if they were clever and struck from within. It wasn't just the public areas that he'd had rigged; the apartments were all wired, too. Which offered the kind of specialised programming you didn't get with conventional cable, even premium rate.

Lucca toggled through the cameras. A lot of the apartments were still empty, but he knew they would fill up and generally the people who took them were young and attractive.

He remembered the couple that had been in the lobby when as he'd left that evening. They were the kind of people he liked to see moving in.

Well, *she* had been.

On the television screen he was looking at a bedroom on the thirteenth floor. Beside the time code at the bottom of the screen another graphic identified the apartment: this was number forty-four. The Lloyd family. Lucca didn't know the names of everyone that had moved into the lower levels of his fortress, but Ewan Lloyd worked for him. He was an accountant, and a good one. He wasn't crooked, but he didn't ask questions.

When Lucca had first met him a year earlier, Ewan Lloyd was a man with a drink problem who could barely afford his next bottle of malt, never mind ask questions. There had been some sort of family trouble that had got him hitting the bottle; Lucca guessed it was something to do with the guy's wife.

Wendy Lloyd was hot. Way too hot for someone like her husband, who was not only a pen-pushing number jockey, but was going bald before he hit forty and carried a belly like a beer keg. Whatever had possessed a woman like her to marry a man like that, it was never going to be long before she strayed. Lucca promised himself a piece of her one day, too, but not until her husband had in some way outlived his usefulness. There were some people that you didn't give a reason to betray you – a good accountant was one of them.

Lloyd had pretty much dried out over the last six months; Lucca guessed that he and Wendy had patched up their marital rift for the sake of their little girl.

Lucca was about to move on from the image of the empty bedroom (as Wendy wasn't slipping out of her clothes in there – and he knew that was a sight not to be missed) when the little girl walked in.

He wasn't much of an expert on kids, but Lucca guessed she was five or six. They called her Alison. She had golden hair like her mum. Lots of it. She'd been lucky, Lucca thought as he watched her climb onto her parents' bed with some kind of big rag doll bundled in her arms. As the cells that had made her had collided inside Wendy Lloyd they had sucked the best part out of her mum's genes and given the finger to the fat, ugly drunk half of the conception. Maybe that kind of genetic deal meant Alison didn't get her dad's brains, either, but Lucca didn't see how that mattered: his interest in women didn't extend to their intellectual abilities. Lucca just hoped Alison's parents stuck around at SkyPoint for another ten years or so.

Alison was sitting on the Lloyds' bed now, cross-legged. She had placed the rag doll opposite her. It looked like it was supposed to be some sort of elf, or goblin or something. It wore a green cap with a bell on the end of it, and there were cloth shoes at the end of its long candy-striped legs that turned up at the toes. It was battered and faded, as if it had been the little girl's companion and confidante her whole life, their only separation being periodic rides in the washing machine.

It sat on the bed with its legs splayed out, its torso bent forward a little to give it some stability. It looked like it was leaning forward, intent on her kiddie conversation. Lucca could see that Alison was filling the doll in on something of vital importance.

Lucca felt something inside him tremble: there was something heartbreaking about the innocence of a child.

Deep down, in a part of him that he rarely visited, Lucca ached. Innocence wouldn't last. The world would see to that.

Lucca switched channels.

He almost missed the guy in the long overcoat.

FIVE

The blonde with the legs who had earlier that afternoon adjusted her neckline for impact had been replaced in the SkyPoint lobby by a grey-suited concierge who probably weighed the equivalent of a fully loaded catering freezer and had the same kind of build.

Jack had checked the guy out as he and Toshiko sat in the SUV parked outside SkyPoint. They could have got past him, but Jack didn't see the sense in drawing attention to their presence when there was always going to be a back door.

As back doors went, when they found it, it was probably one of the most secure Jack had ever seen, with the kind of digital lock you normally found on the airlock of a bio-hazard lab.

'If I was a burglar, I'd look somewhere else,' Toshiko muttered as she ran her eye over the lock, then placed a gadget from her messenger bag against it.

The back door sprang open.

'If the Rift ever closes down, I can see a whole new career for you,' smiled Jack.

Toshiko glanced at Jack. 'Yes. Well, I have form, don't I?'

Jack felt his smile shrivel. He had recruited Toshiko into Torchwood from a UNIT cell that hadn't been big enough to lie down in after she had stolen classified plans for an experimental weapon. She had been coerced into the theft by terrorists who kidnapped her mother, but the price of springing her from the military jail had included severing contact with her family. He had given Toshiko her freedom, but freedom was a relative concept when you worked for Torchwood.

He led the way into the apartment building and Toshiko followed, closing the door gently behind them. They found an elevator and rode it to the tenth floor.

As the doors opened on the passageway, Toshiko took out another hand-held piece of tech. It flickered with liquid-crystal graphics.

'No sign of Rift activity,' she said, as they moved along the passageway and Jack scanned the doors for the apartment Gwen and Rhys had visited earlier that day.

'What about residual energy?'

'Nothing showing.'

Jack frowned. 'Well, I don't have a whole lot of experience in real estate, but the way I hear it those guys don't generally walk out on a potential sale.'

'I can only tell you what my instruments are showing, Jack.'

He nodded, accepting Toshiko's findings, but not in the least bit comforted by them. They had reached the door they were looking for, and Jack stood aside to let her work her magic on the lock. Moments later, they were inside, the apartment's movement detectors activating the lights for them.

'Wow. This is nice,' Toshiko purred, taking the apartment in.

'Sure beats my place,' Jack smiled, moving to the window and looking out across night-lit Cardiff. Home for Jack was little more than a cell in the bowels of the Hub. But then he wasn't big on home comforts.

He spun away from the window and headed for the master bedroom. 'Gwen said the guy vanished from the en suite bathroom, right?'

Toshiko followed, just two steps behind and reached the bedroom as Jack dived onto the massive bed in there like a big kid.

'Now *this* is something I could use,' he grinned.

Toshiko smiled. Jack was a big kid sometimes, all right, but he didn't play kids' games. She bet he could come up with some pretty interesting and enjoyable ways to use the bed.

For a nano-second she wondered if he was about to invite her to try out a couple, and she wondered if she would agree. Then he was off the bed, and springing towards the bathroom where the estate agent had vanished.

'No obvious escape routes,' he said, running his eyes over the stylish slate and granite. 'Apart from the obvious,' as he looked at the toilet.

He raised the seat and glanced into the bowl. 'Nope. Nothing here.'

Toshiko ran her instrument around the bathroom. Again, the graphics gave no indication of Rift activity.

'It doesn't make sense,' she said. 'People just don't disappear.'

'Actually people disappear all the time, Tosh. But there's always a reason for it.'

'Well the reason for this can't be the Rift.' She stowed her kit in the messenger bag.

'So what do you suggest?'

'There are possibilities. Teleportation.'

'And who would want to teleport an estate agent?'

'OK, then... Maybe he was never here.'

'Gwen and Rhys imagined him? You're going to have to try harder than that,' Jack smiled as he headed back into the bedroom.

Toshiko followed him. 'I'm just going through the logical—'

She didn't get any further. The sight of the concierge built like an industrial freezer stopped her.

He was standing in the bedroom, waiting for them.

'What are you doing in here?' the concierge asked with a voice that sounded like ice cubes being crushed.

Jack shrugged and gave the industrial freezer guy one of his smiles. 'Looking for an apartment.'

The smile didn't work, neither did the answer. The concierge looked at Jack with steel grey eyes that had about as much life in them as a mortuary slab.

'Who are you?' he asked.

Toshiko noticed a thin curled wire that fed upwards from the concierge's collar into an earpiece. She decided that the questions were coming from someplace else. He obviously didn't draw his pay cheque on his intellectual qualities.

Jack gave the guy another smile. Not the high-beam dazzle-and-run smile; this one was lower intensity, the kind that drew you in and suckered you. Jack had a million smiles. One time, somewhere, Jack had been some sort of con man. She guessed that was how he came by the Smiles.

As he smiled at the industrial freezer guy, he also moved towards him, his hands opening wide in a gesture of coming clean. His voice came down a little, like a guy with something to admit, guy-to-guy.

'Thing is,' Jack was telling the concierge, 'my girlfriend and me, we have this thing. About doing it in show homes. You get me?'

The concierge looked from Jack to Toshiko.

Toshiko tried her best not to look shocked by Jack's suggestion. And she saw the slightest kink of a smile on the concierge's thin lips. It didn't make him look any more friendly.

'I'm telling you, we've done it everywhere. Not just show homes, either. A couple of times we've let people selling their house show us around then asked for a few minutes alone just to talk it over, you know? And…' Jack gave the concierge a friendly nudge.

'So this place… well, this is like the Mile High Club for us. Anyway, we're done now, so we'll get off the premises. OK?'

Jack started to head for the door, but the concierge dropped one big hand on his shoulder.

'No. You're coming with me.'

'Look,' Toshiko said, 'there's no need to involve the police. We'll just leave quietly.'

The concierge looked at her with his mortuary steel eyes and she knew he wasn't about to involve the police anyway.

'You're coming with me,' he said again.

'Whatever you say,' Jack told him, and took Toshiko's hand, playing the boyfriend. 'Come on, babe.'

Toshiko shot him a glance – *babe?!* – and Jack felt the concierge's hand between his shoulder blades push him towards the door.

As he and Toshiko stepped through it, the bedroom door slammed shut behind them with a sound like a gunshot.

Jack and Toshiko spun around.

The door trembled on its hinges for a moment, as if someone on the other side were hammering and kicking on it.

But there was no sound.

And then the trembling stopped.

Toshiko and Jack looked at each other.

Jack drew the Webley service revolver from his belt.

Toshiko pulled the Glock automatic from the shoulder holster hidden beneath her jacket. At the same time, she removed the Rift detector from her bag.

Jack threw her a glance. Her eyes told him she was ready. His hand twisted the door handle. And together they stepped back into the bedroom.

The empty bedroom.

Toshiko checked the bathroom, and Jack checked the dressing area. But there was no sign of the freezer-sized concierge. And there was nothing registering on Toshiko's equipment.

'I say we get out of here,' said Jack.

And they did.

And in his penthouse Besnik Lucca watched it all.

SIX

There had been a time in his life when Owen Harper had done everything he could to fight sleep. He had lost count of the pills he had put down his neck to help keep it at bay. As a doctor, he understood the importance of sleep; as a man he resented the chunks of life that it stole from him. Perhaps on some level he had always known that his life would be cut short and had been driven by his subconscious to make the most of what time he had. What he could never have imagined was that, at the age of twenty-six, he would have his heart reduced to mincemeat, and yet he would carry on living; nor that, in that twilight of half-life that he now endured, he would ache so much for the intermittent release of sleep.

But just as there was no rest for the wicked, as his grandmother used to tell him (God bless her mercifully departed soul) there was apparently no sleep for the undead. And when booze just filled your belly till it swelled up like an overfilled waterbed and the only way of getting rid of it was to stand on your head, open your oesophagus and wait for it to flood out across the floor around you, there wasn't much point in filling the small hours with endless partying. And since blood no longer pumped around his body, the fuel line had run out on sex.

If Owen had believed in reincarnation – and it was odd that being dead his views on religion and the possibilities of an afterlife hadn't really changed at all (he just didn't buy into any of it) – but if there had been any such thing as karma then, by Christ, he must have really pissed off the gods in some past life. When he'd been a junior doctor doing his time in the genito-urinary department, he had met guys who couldn't get it up. And that to Owen was a walking death in itself. If there was such a thing as karma and the shot that Pharm bastard Aaron Copley had fired through his heart was cosmic payback for stamping on a beetle when he was Genghis Khan or something, then there really wasn't any need to go the whole hog. Not being able to have sex, but still aching for it was the most relentless, torturous punishment Owen could think of. Those hooded characters in the Middle Ages with their red hot pokers had nothing on this!

He had taken out a membership card at a DVD rental store and he was probably their best customer: three movies generally got him through the worst part of the night. Trouble was, he'd already gone through most of the good ones. The tag line on one of them – a lousy vampire flick with too many bare bouncing breasts that had only served to remind him of what he was missing – had purred *It's cool to be a vampire.* Well, a vampire was the walking dead like him, and Owen found it pretty bloody hard to come up with anything – any damned thing at all – that was in any way cool about being dead and still walking.

But he supposed that was Hollywood for you. If you asked an American movie producer, John Wayne won the war single-handed; Robin Hood was a Yank with thinning hair and the White Cliffs of Dover were a five-minute walk from Nottingham Forest; and the crew of the Titanic passed the last few minutes of their lives shooting the passengers. Vampires probably felt pretty pissed off with the rep they got from Hollywood, too. Maybe that was why they were sometimes known as Nightwalkers because, as Owen had discovered, when you were dead but the message hadn't got through to your body, walking was pretty much all there was left to do.

So that was how Owen Harper spent the hours when decent folk went to sleep, and the not-so-decent partied.

And as miserable an existence as it was, being undead, Owen couldn't help smiling at the irony of the situation. He spent hours every night walking the streets of Cardiff. He had already worn through two pairs of shoes. If he were still alive, he'd have been the fittest he'd ever been. He couldn't drink, he couldn't eat, and he couldn't shag – but at least he still had his sense of humour.

Always look on the bright side of death, as Eric Idle had said.

Yeah, well maybe he wasn't quite that relaxed about it. And he didn't think he ever would be. But at least Torchwood was still paying him, dead or alive. That would keep him in shoe leather and it looked like he was going to need it.

Come to that, now he didn't need to eat and he couldn't

drink and heating in his flat wasn't really much of an issue as he could feel neither cold nor heat, his wages were starting to stack up in the bank. Another of the ironies of a living death.

He did still buy the occasional coffee, however. Like now. He never drank it. It just went cold in the cup before him, but people were used to people sitting over drinks that they hardly touched in all-night cafés like this one. The staff left you alone with your demons. At 2am on a Tuesday morning, if you weren't some sort of shift worker looking for a caffeine buzz to get you through the night and you were hunched over a coffee in a dive like Constantine's, chances were you had demons of one sort or another.

And it was demons of a kind that had brought Owen here tonight and every night for the last three weeks.

But they weren't his.

Except that he had kind of made them his own by deciding not to tell the rest of the team about the man he had seen ripped to pieces by two women in an alleyway at the back of the café.

They weren't really women, of course. As the two of them had torn the poor guy apart like two halves of a butchered pig, their jaws had distended and expanded and the small pearl teeth that they had flashed at the poor sod just a few minutes before grew into razor-edged spikes. Their flesh had turned to scales. Their eyes had grown large and black, like those of a dead shark.

Owen watched it all from the cover of a dumpster that stank of rotting food, and the odour of a drunk's toilet. The man had been dead before Owen got there – the girls were pragmatic butchers: they had taken off their victim's head first, effectively stemming any cries for help and killing him at once. By the time Owen had reached the cover of the dumpster, the guy had been nothing but dead meat and bone – and the two creatures had devoured it all, ripped dripping red flesh from living bone then ground the broken skeleton between their massive, powerful extended jaws. The sound of the dead man's bones being pulverised and devoured was loud and industrial, like machinery rendering waste.

Thirty minutes earlier, Owen had watched the girls walk into Constantine's coffee shop. They had smiled at him as they came through the door. They had looked at him in the same beat and both had curved and parted their lips a moment later and shown him small, perfectly white teeth as if on cue. Each smile was an exact copy of the other. And the girls almost were.

Twins, Owen had thought, and he felt that hopelessly familiar ache for the things he would have done before that bastard's bullet put an end to more than just his life. As fantasies went, twins were right up there. And Owen had fulfilled most of his fantasies generally more than once with a succession of women. But he had never made it with twins. And he was never going to. That was why he looked away from the girls as they smiled his way, and that was probably why they moved on.

All the same, Owen was curious and he watched them in the night-time mirror-glass of the big coffee shop window as the twins bought cappuccinos from the bag-eyed student who did the Constantine's nightshift three days a week.

They couldn't have been much past eighteen; they were

tall – maybe five-eight (and most of that was leg) with the lean, toned bodies of athletes – and they dressed in duplicate red outfits that displayed a lot of chest and lot of thigh. Each wore white boots.

Clubbers, Owen guessed. The only difference between them was their hair. Both wore it long, but one was black, the other was the colour of bleached silver. If they pulled (and why the hell wouldn't they?) it was the only way their guys would tell them apart. And they were probably wigs that the girls switched in the toilets to have fun with their unsuspecting dates. They looked like a couple of girls who liked to have fun.

Boy, he thought later, didn't he get that right.

But dressed like that at this time in this part of town was asking for trouble. There were five other guys in the coffee shop apart from Owen and the student barista. Owen wouldn't have trusted any of them with his dog, never mind his daughter. All of them watched the girls as they waited for the coffees, and the girls spent the time leaning their slender backs against the counter watching the men. Occasionally one would whisper to the other, and the other would snigger, flashing a glance at one of the men who would know beyond doubt that they were discussing him. Owen knew how that would feel and these girls were playing with fire. Either they had just escaped from a convent school, or they knew exactly what they were doing.

Owen's worries for the safety of the girls began to subside. He started to worry about the men.

The student behind the bar put the girls' coffees on the stained and scarred stainless-steel counter and Owen watched as they turned and reached for drinks in perfect unison.

Unnatural unison.

And together, without discussion, they took a table next to a man in his middle thirties. His hair was long, tied back in a ponytail. He hadn't shaved in a couple of days but his clothes were clean and no shabbier than your regular Cardiff student. Like the rest of the men in there, he hadn't failed to notice the twins, but he'd shared his interest in them with the book he was reading. Or, more likely, had the discretion to hide it behind the book. Owen couldn't see what the book was, but it looked like some sort of paperback academia. The guy was probably a mature student, or maybe a lecturer. As the girls sat down, they both flashed the ponytailed guy those white smiles, and in them Owen recognised just the right proportions of shyness, interest and promise. Like they had used a formula to work it out.

Only the guy with the ponytail and the highbrow paperback would never see that.

Didn't matter how bright a man was, when a sexy woman smiled at you – that was all you saw. When you were looking at twin smiles that glowed like that, it was like being hit by closing car headlights and suddenly you were no better than a dumb rabbit.

When the man smiled back, Owen knew the guy was dead. Whatever the twins really were inside the flesh that they wore so well as they worked the men in the coffee shop, they were predators. And Owen watched, fascinated, as they stalked their prey across the half-dried puddles of cold coffee on the old scratched table. All it really needed was David Attenborough whispering a commentary in his ear.

He wasn't close enough to hear what the women said to the ponytailed student/lecturer, all he could do was read the body language, but it wasn't a long dialogue. Just a few minutes later all three were pushing back their chairs and moving towards the coffee-shop door and the darkness that waited outside. Owen watched them in the window, and started to work out what he was going to do. Fascination with these hunting creatures was one thing, they had provided a distraction from his nocturnal boredom, but he couldn't let this go the whole way...

As they passed him and opened the door onto the street Owen could feel the heat of excitement coming off the ponytailed guy. If he'd looked, Owen was sure he'd have seen it building up in the guy's crotch. Owen let them slip through the door, and the girls were laughing at something the guy had just said. Their laughter made Owen think of Disney fairies; it was delicate and musical and unreal. As the door closed behind them it cut the sound off. Owen watched them turn left, one twin either side of the student/lecturer as he slipped an arm around each girl's waist. Then Owen slid off his chair and headed after them. He checked for the automatic tucked into the back of his belt; his hand was still busted from that bad night with Toshiko a few weeks back (it would always be busted since his body no longer had the ability to heal), but he knew he could still handle the gun OK. He didn't really want to use it on the two pretty girls, but Torchwood had given him a pretty reliable sense about things around Cardiff, especially at this time of night, when things that looked a little odd were, in reality, probably right off the scale. He didn't want to shoot the two girls, but he knew that was not what they were.

As he opened the door, a drunk the size of a grizzly bear lurched through it off the street and waded blindly into Owen on rubber legs. Something unintelligible slipped out of the drunk's mouth as his eyes scrambled for focus and gave up. Owen thought it might have been an apology, and told the drunk that it was OK, then tried to get around him and out of the door, but the drunk clapped a meaty shovel of a hand against Owen's shoulder and said something else, his eyes still swirling in his head like a couple of goldfish in twin bowls.

V gt nmney. Lsst't. Cnn yuu…

Owen told the drunk that he didn't have time for this, but the drunk wasn't listening. He put his other hand on Owen's other shoulder, and Owen wasn't sure if the guy was trying to fix him with a look or just trying to stand up.

Y'lk lk nss kndablk…

And the guy with the ponytail and the two sexy girls that were something else entirely were getting further and further away…

Owen really didn't have time for this.

He kicked the drunk hard just under the kneecap and the guy went down like a detonated apartment block. Owen was out on the street a moment later, and turned left but there was no sign of the ponytailed guy or the two women.

Shit.

Owen ran. He knew they couldn't have gone far, but around here it was a maze of backstreets and alleyways. Each one was a black hole that could hide anything. Owen took the first one he came to. Logic suggested that was what they would have done. He pulled the gun from where it nestled in the small of his back and moved into the darkness of the alleyway, creeping quickly but silently. One thing about being dead, you never ran out of breath.

That was when Owen had seen that he was too late to save the man with the ponytail, and he had taken cover behind the dumpster, overcome by sick fascination as he watched the two women-things devour him, bones and all.

It was over in no more than five minutes – the girls killed and ate with a bloody choreography that was both practised and obscenely natural – but the worst part came at the end.

As they finished their feast, the girls' alien transformation went into reverse as if it had been a reaction to their hungry bloodlust and now, sated, the spikes, scales and crunching jaws were shrinking away, the monsters metamorphosing back into the slight, vulnerable young women Owen had seen walk into the coffee shop. Only now they were on their knees in the filth of the back alley, licking up the blood and last remains of their victim from the dirt-encrusted paving and from his shredded clothing that was now all that remained of the man that had been drinking a two-shot white Americano in Constantine's just a few minutes earlier. But that wasn't the worst part.

Owen watched in fascinated horror as the slighter of the girls held a ragged strip of shirt linen in both hands and licked the blood off it the way people lick a yoghurt lid clean. Then, together, they gathered the dead man's clothes and moved towards the dumpster with them.

Owen sank back further into the shadows. For a moment he forgot he was dead and tried to hold his breath.

They threw the savaged bundle of rags into the bin, and then came the worst part of all. The really bad bit – that was worse than any amount of flesh-tearing, bone crunching and blood-licking. The part that made Owen grateful that he no longer slept, that he would never have dreams that could be haunted by what he heard as the two women held hands and walked off into the darkness.

Their laughter. Musical and ethereal. And enough to chill a dead man's bones.

Owen didn't move from the darkness from behind the dumpster for maybe a full minute. And when he did, he looked down into his hand and saw that he still held the automatic, fully loaded, not a shot fired.

Why didn't you use the gun?

And he didn't know what scared him the most.

That was why he had kept what he had seen to himself. When morning came, he had gone to the Hub, seen Jack, Ianto and Toshiko and he hadn't said a word. But that night he had returned to Constantine's and he had waited for the twins to show up. They hadn't, but Owen knew that they would. Some time. They were hunters and hunters always returned to the site of a good kill. Lions hunted at waterholes, these things stalked bars and coffee shops.

A couple of days later, the Hub's computer system picked up a missing persons report on the Cardiff police system. Owen recognised the guy with the ponytail. Jean-Claude Gabin, a French philosophy student. He had been reported missing by his flatmate. The police had so far failed to find any trace of him. Owen doubted that they would. But people went missing all the time, and most of them turned up again safe and sound – even in Cardiff. Jean-Claude Gabin wouldn't show up on the Torchwood radar unless parts of him showed up in the gutter, and the twins had been too fastidious for that.

So that night Owen had walked the streets of Cardiff once more until daybreak. And he had spent hours bent over a cooling, and cold, mug of coffee in Constantine's. But the twins hadn't shown up again.

And tonight he was here again.

For all he knew – or cared – the kid behind the bar could be just putting the same cold Americano in front of him that Owen had been bent over for the last week as he waited.

All that mattered was that he was there when the twins returned.

SEVEN

Goldman and Grace had offices that looked out on the Castle. Jack Harkness stood before the estate agent's massive window that was filled with colour photographs of the city's prime housing market – much of it located high up in the sky – and his eyes roved across the interior shots of stylish twenty-first-century accommodation to the looming presence of the Castle reflected in the glass from behind him. This was where ancient Cardiff met the modern city, in an estate agent's window. It was kind of fitting, he thought. And then his eyes roved some more, and found his own reflection.

Not bad.

Not bad at all, considering all that he had been through over the years.

And there had been a lot of years for Jack Harkness. He had decided to quit counting them a long time ago. Time hadn't held the relevance for Jack that it had for most people in a very long... well, time.

It was one of the first things you revised your opinion on when you were a Time Agent, and your work took you across galaxies and aeons, and it was a tough job to work out which was the cooler.

Eventually, however, he had wound up in London in 1941. The Blitz. He and the Time Agency had had a parting of the ways by then, and Jack was more of a lone operator doing what he had always done best – taking care of himself. And that had been when he had met the man that was going to change his life. And, pretty soon after, the concept of time and the point of counting it in years, even centuries was going to come pretty low among Jack's priorities.

Jack had decided that when you couldn't die, it was best not to keep count of the years. For one thing, there was no need: the counting of time was, after all, just a measurement of mortality. For another thing, it was the best way of keeping sane.

So Jack didn't worry about the passing years, he just tried to get on with enjoying immortality.

'If you've finished admiring yourself, shall we go in now?'

The voice lanced through Jack's thoughts. And he saw himself smile in the window, the pictures of modern Cardiff before him, the ancient Castle behind him, and Gwen Cooper – no, *Williams* – beside him. He reminded himself that he was going to have to get used to that new second name. Marriage, he thought, was good for her. She was lovelier than ever.

'You know,' he told her, 'Rhys is a lucky man, Mrs Williams.'

Gwen froze and stared at him. She blinked, then took out her mobile phone, her gaze never leaving his.

'Rhys? Hi… No, everything's… Yeah, later… Yeah, lovely… No, it's… Look, Rhys, will you stop a minute? Thanks. It's just…' She paused, took a breath. 'It's just I've been thinking, love, and I've decided I'll be keeping my own name. You know, for work and that. It's not that I… What?'

She listened for a moment, then broke out in a huge grin.

'I love you, Rhys Williams.' She switched off her phone.

'What'd he say?' Jack asked.

'He said, "Yeah, I know that, love."' Gwen beamed back at Jack.

And maybe that was what Jack needed. Confirmation that she was happy, that she knew she had done the right thing a little over two weeks ago.

Jack smiled. 'Let's go see what they've got to say about your disappearing estate agent, PC Cooper,' he said, and he opened the glass door for her to go into the showroom ahead of him.

Gwen swept into the front office of Goldman and Grace, Jack close behind her, and together they took the place in. Nothing extraordinary. Jack had lived in the Hub for a long time, and they didn't have estate agents where he came from in the fifty-first century, so he didn't have a whole lot of experience on which to judge, but he guessed this was par for the course. Good photographs, well presented; relevant details, clearly arranged. The same went for the staff: well presented and clearly arranged. And it didn't take long for one of them to settle on the new arrivals – not like a bird of prey, more like a blackbird delicately probing for nourishment.

'Can I help you?' the blackbird enquired.

It was a tall woman in her late forties, dressed elegantly. She was smiling, and it was almost convincing. But not quite.

Jack let Gwen open the business. She was the cop, after all.

Gwen gave the blackbird her own smile. 'Hi. What's your name?'

The blackbird's smile faltered a little. People usually told her they were looking for two or three bedrooms, or somewhere with a garden, they didn't ask her name.

'Jan,' the woman said.

'Well, Jan, we're making enquiries about a colleague of yours. Brian Shaw.'

Gwen saw the defences go up around Jan like the USS *Enterprise* on red alert.

'What sort of enquiries. Who are you?'

Jack saw one of the SkyPoint brochures and started flicking through it. He made it look like idle curiosity. At the same time he said, 'Is he about?'

'It's his day off,' she said.

'You sure about that?' he asked.

'Look, what is this? If you're the police I'd like to see some ID.'

But Jack hadn't finished. 'You see, the way we hear it, he's disappeared.'

'I really don't know what you think you're playing at, but if you don't leave I'm going to call the police.' And Jan picked up the closest phone to prove she meant business.

The phone was on the desk of a guy of about twenty. He had ginger hair, and a razor nick on his neck. There was a corresponding tiny smear of blood on his collar, which Gwen judged was a size too big for him. The office junior, she guessed. And she caught his eye for a moment. She read the anxiety there.

'Call the police if you like, Jan,' Jack told her. 'When you do, be sure to mention the word Torchwood. They'll appreciate it. It'll save them a wasted journey.'

Jan was out of her depth. Luckily, she had a lifeguard. He came in a pinstriped suit and had silver whiskers and his name was Grace.

'I'll handle this, Jan.'

Jack and Gwen turned to see the pinstriped man in the doorway of a back office. As they did so, he went into smiling mode. With him, it went with an offered manicured hand.

'Arwen Grace,' he said. 'This is my business. How can I help you, Mister...?'

Jack took the man's hand and shook it. 'Harkness. Jack. Captain.'

'A services man,' Grace noted with pleasure. 'I did twenty years in the navy. I take it that you were a flyer.'

'Of sorts.'

Gwen felt excluded from the club.

'Gwen Cooper,' she said, projecting her hand.

Grace shook it and smiled. He said he was charmed. And Gwen recognised the tone. He may have been charmed, but Gwen knew when she was being disregarded.

Grace indicated for them to follow him and led them

into a comfortable if old-fashioned office. As he closed the door behind them, Gwen caught the ginger-haired guy she'd taken for the office junior watching them. And she recognised the look. She had seen it plenty of times before when she'd done the Cardiff beat. It was a look you learned quickly as a cop – of someone who knows something, but is too scared to talk.

'The fact of the matter,' Grace was telling them, 'is that Brian Shaw has a few problems.'

Yeah, like vanishing into thin air.

But Gwen kept her mouth shut.

Jack had eased himself into the heavily padded leather chair that stood opposite the big antique desk the estate agent now moved behind. Gwen stood by the door with her arms folded. She wanted Grace to know that she wasn't getting sucked in by his show of hospitality.

'Personal problems,' Grace clarified.

'So you know where he is, then?' Jack asked.

Grace took his seat behind the desk and leaned forward, sliding his fingers into a latticed bunch before him on his blotter. 'I'm afraid Brian likes a drink a little more than is good for him. This line of work is extremely high-pressured. Not everyone can take it. Even those who are good at it go through their lean periods.'

'I thought the property market had been going through the roof,' Gwen said, and she knew it sounded a little like an accusation.

The estate agent cast her a benevolent smile. 'Cardiff is a boom town, there's no doubt about that. Developers are pouring money into building projects like there's no tomorrow. The problem is that there are so many apartments going up, and the banks are falling over themselves to lend money, buyers are being spoiled for choice. I'm afraid the sharks are turning on one another amid a feeding frenzy of minnows.'

'You're saying Brian Shaw is under pressure.'

'That's right, Captain Harkness. And when under pressure, he normally ends up under a table somewhere. I've seen it before. We all have.'

'When was the last time you spoke to Brian Shaw?' asked Gwen.

Grace didn't even have to think about it. 'Yesterday evening. Seven o'clock. When we closed the office.'

Gwen glanced at Jack. He knew it, too: Grace was lying.

'He had already been drinking,' Grace continued. 'I could smell it on his breath. I know how it goes with Brian. I like him, otherwise I would have sacked him a long time ago. But he'll be on a bender for a couple of days, he'll get it all out of his system, and then he'll start selling like the devil's on his tail.'

Jack got out of the chair and moved across the office to a picture on the wall – it was SkyPoint. 'That's kind of interesting, Mr Grace. You see we've got a report that Brian Shaw disappeared in the middle of showing a couple around an apartment here.'

Jack cocked a thumb at the picture of SkyPoint.

'And when I say disappeared, I mean the way a magician does it. Now you see him, now you don't.'

Gwen noticed Grace shift in his seat.

'I don't follow you,' he said.

Gwen decided to show him the way. 'He walked into a bathroom, and then he wasn't there any more. There was no way he could have got out without being seen.'

'Maybe we should go and talk to Brian ourselves,' Jack said from over by the SkyPoint picture. 'Maybe that's the easiest way of clearing this up. You've got an address for him, haven't you, Mr Grace?'

Gwen was nodding. 'That's a good idea. We can ask him how he managed to be here at seven last night when that was just about the time I saw him walk into the bathroom in apartment thirty-two and disappear.'

Grace shot her a look. 'You were there?'

'Want to change your story, Mr Grace?' she asked.

His eyes snapped from Gwen to Jack, and back. He shook his head. His skin had turned to something like the colour of his whiskers. Gwen had seen this look before, as well. It was the look of a frightened man.

'You're mistaken,' Grace said, his voice now little more than a whisper.

Jack strode across the room. 'Thank you, Mr Grace. You've told us everything we needed to know.'

And Jack yanked the office door open and left. As Gwen followed him, she saw Grace's eyes moving towards the telephone on his desk. He was going to have to ring someone, she thought, someone he didn't want to talk to. She was going to have a job for Toshiko when she got back to the Hub.

As she followed Jack across the front office towards the street, she noticed that the ginger-haired guy was missing from his seat.

'*Everything we needed to know?*' she demanded as she caught up with Jack outside.

'Well, we found out that he wasn't going to talk. That tells us something. Whatever happened to Brian Shaw, this is about more than just a disappearing estate agent.'

They rounded a corner and found the black SUV where Jack had left it, parked outside the Hilton. Jack gave the young doorman a familiar smile. 'Everything OK, Simon?'

The doorman smiled back. 'I know you, Jack Harkness, you only want me for my parking facility.'

Jack grinned. 'Well, you're handy when I'm carrying a heavy load. I know you'll take care of it for me.'

Gwen tuned out of Jack's flirting, and spotted the ginger-headed office junior watching them. He was still looking anxious. More than ever. Gwen started to move towards him, treading carefully like he was a small animal ready to run for cover.

'Hello,' she said. 'Do you want to talk?'

The office junior had one last second thought – she could actually see it pass through his mind, as his eyes flashed past her, charting an escape route – then he asked her, 'What did the old man tell you about Brian?'

'Well, I don't think he told us the truth.'

'He isn't off on a bender. I'd know if he was. The old man, he doesn't know, but me and Brian we're… friends. I'd know if he was feeling the strain, he'd have told me. The old man is covering up.'

'Covering what up?' Gwen asked. Behind her, Jack had seen her with the office junior and was joining them.

The office junior hesitated.

'It's OK, you can trust us,' Jack told him. 'Whatever it is, just spit it out.'

'It's that place. SkyPoint.'

'What about it?' asked Gwen.

'They're trying to keep it quiet. The place cost millions and it's still more than three-quarters empty. If word got out about the people disappearing there—'

'People?' Jack snapped. 'Brian Shaw isn't the first? This has happened before?'

The office junior flashed an uneasy look around him, scanned the street for faces that he knew, anyone from work. 'Christ, if anyone finds out I talked to you…'

'I understand you're worried about your job,' Gwen told him, 'but you have to tell us what you know.'

The junior shook his head. 'My job? There's plenty of jobs. It's my neck I'm worried about. You don't know the kind of people that have got money in SkyPoint.'

Gwen remembered the man that lived in the penthouse. 'Besnik Lucca?'

'Yeah, well then, you know what I'm talking about. Men like that want to see a return on their investment. It doesn't matter to them that there's something *wrong* with the place.'

'So how many people are we talking about?' Jack wanted to know. 'How many have disappeared?'

'Four that I know of. Not counting Brian. At first we thought it was just people running out on their payments, but not one of them was caught by the security cameras leaving. And those cameras spot everyone going into SkyPoint and coming out. The only way you can get out of that place without being picked up on video is jumping off the roof.'

'Well, if they'd done that, you'd know about it,' said Jack, dry as sand.

The office junior looked from Jack to Gwen, confused and scared. 'Where do they go? Where's Brian gone?'

Gwen touched his shoulder gently. 'We're going to find out. I promise you.'

EIGHT

Ianto Jones took his coffee black, and seriously.

When Torchwood One had been destroyed in the Battle of Canary Wharf, Ianto had been one of the few survivors, and he had returned to Wales looking for a job with the Cardiff operation. Jack had never had much time for Torchwood One, he didn't like the way they did things and thought their disastrous handling of the Dalek-Cyberman situation had proved him right. So he was never going to have much interest in Ianto Jones, despite the cut of his suit, never mind how cute he might have been. But Ianto was determined, and he campaigned hard, though to Jack it felt like he'd got himself a stalker. And Ianto was ready to do anything to get himself a place in the Hub. He was an intelligent man with Honours in English Literature and History – but he'd just make the coffee and run the hoover around if that was what it took to get back into Torchwood.

So, in the end, Jack had given him a break as the tea boy and the guy who rang for the pizzas. He had earned his stripes since then and no one really thought of him as the office boy any more. He was a lot more than that, especially to Jack. But no one else could make coffee like Ianto. And, truth was, Ianto liked to make coffee. There was more to it than pouring hot water over ground beans.

The philosopher Sir James Mackintosh had said that the powers of a man's mind were proportionate to the quantity of coffee he drank, and Voltaire had knocked back fifty cups of it a day, so Ianto reckoned there had to be something in it. And saving Cardiff from the kinds of things that came through the Rift called for quick, inspired thinking, so Ianto took it upon himself to make sure the coffee was good.

Ianto Jones, saving the world with a dark roast.

And that was what he set down on the conference room table now. A tray of four mugs. Dark Java.

He handed the drinks around as people talked, worked out how they were going to handle SkyPoint, how they were going to find out what was going on there.

'What have you got, Tosh?' Jack asked as Ianto put a coffee mug in his hand.

Toshiko referred to the notes from her computer research that morning. 'SkyPoint is built on the site of old dock warehousing. I've gone back as far as I can, but there are no records of Rift activity in the location. So no historical precedent for what seems to be happening there now.'

'And no records of disappearances?' Jack asked.

'Not specific to that site. Not that I can see.'

'So this is something to do with the building itself,' Owen pondered as he watched Ianto hand the coffees around. He remembered that Ianto made good coffee – better than the shit they stung you more than two quid for down at Constantine's, anyway, he guessed.

'So there's – what? – some creature living in there?' Ianto suggested as he sat down at the table and took the first sip of Java. It was good. Of course it was.

'Something that consumes people? Doesn't leave a trace of them behind?' Owen heard what he was saying and worried. If the thing in SkyPoint was the same thing that he had seen butcher the French philosophy student and then clean up afterwards better than those two old birds in rubber gloves on the telly – then he had to come clean to the rest of the team.

But Gwen didn't think that was it. 'There wasn't time. Rhys and me, we were only seconds behind Brian Shaw when he walked into the bathroom. If it was some sort of creature, we would have heard something. No way that we wouldn't.'

'And we didn't hear anything like a creature when the security guy disappeared, either,' said Toshiko.

Jack pushed back his chair and started to prowl around the table. 'So what happened? They didn't get beamed up by Mr Scott. And, as far as our instruments can tell, there's no Rift activity, so they didn't just get sucked out of existence.'

Gwen shook her head. 'But it has to be the Rift.'

Jack came to a stop; he'd done a full turn of the table and was back behind his own chair. He put his fists on his hips.

'There's only one way we're going to find out,' he said. 'Who wants to play Happy Families?'

NINE

This is going to be weird.

Owen was standing at the window of his new apartment looking across the Bay. The open-plan SkyPoint living area was filled with unopened boxes. There was no urgency in opening them – most had just been packed with old books to perfect the illusion of a couple moving into their new home.

A couple.

This was going to be very weird, he thought, and looked out across the water wondering just how the hell he was going to get through this.

'Well, that's me all moved in.'

Owen turned from the window as Toshiko walked in from the bedroom. She was dressed in jeans and a thin sweater that clung to her tightly. She had her hair tied back in a ponytail. Owen guessed that this was what she looked like on a day off and realised with surprise that he had never actually seen Toshiko on a day off. She looked like a woman would the day she moved into her new apartment. She looked good. But that wasn't going to make any of this anything like easier.

'It's a walk-in wardrobe,' she told him. 'I hung all my stuff on the right. You can have the left.'

'No problem,' Owen said. 'I dress on the left, anyway.'

Toshiko didn't look like she got the joke.

'I'll hang my stuff up later,' he said. 'Want a coffee?'

'Great,' she said. Her eyes sparkled.

Owen crossed into the kitchen area and filled the kettle, then took a mug from the box of kitchen things that Ianto had put together for them. The mugs were stylish, tall and slim with silver rims. Very Ianto. Back in Owen's apartment, the mugs he drank from (*whoa – hold that! – the mugs he used to drink from*) were a mostly chipped and tea-stained collection that looked like they had been accrued over the years from visiting workmen.

He set one mug down on the work surface and set about working out the high-tech coffee machine that came with the kitchen. Ianto had packed them a full dinner service – the works, in fact – but they were never going to be setting more than one place for dinner here. Owen guessed it would save on the washing up. Six plates, six sets of cutlery – with luck he would be out of SkyPoint before the dishwasher was half full.

He got the coffee machine working and suddenly the apartment was filled with music. Jazz. The Dave Brubeck Quartet. Owen looked across the room and saw Toshiko at the apartment's sound system. Music seemed to pour out of every corner of the apartment.

She was swaying with the rhythm of 'Love For Sale', and caught Owen watching her. Suddenly self-conscious she smiled and turned the music down a little.

'I'm sorry. Do you mind?' she asked.

Owen shrugged and couldn't help smiling. 'I didn't know you liked jazz.'

'My mother's a big fan. It used to be on all the time when I was growing up.'

'Same here. I used to think it was the only thing that stopped my folks going for each other with the kitchen knives. "Take Five" would chill them out better than a case of red.'

'Sorry. If it brings back memories...'

She moved to turn it off.

'No. I like it. Like you said, it rubs off on you.'

Toshiko shook her head. 'It's weird, isn't it? We spend all that time with each other and we go through all this stuff – but we know next to nothing about everyone else.'

Owen stiffened. 'Yeah, well maybe it's better that way.'

'I don't understand.'

'You know what it's like, Tosh. No one gets to retire from Torchwood. And it isn't worth taking out a pension plan.'

She knew what he was talking about. She had gone back through the Torchwood records once. No one had ever left the organisation for another job, or to start a family, or to go live in a cottage by the sea. Personnel files all closed with the same word: DECEASED.

But Toshiko didn't want to think about that. She forced a smile. 'You're a bundle of joy today.'

Owen fought down the urge to tell her that he didn't get

the opportunity for much joy these days. He wondered whether he should also remind her that they were at SkyPoint to do a job, and that they were not there playing House.

Owen's heart may have stopped beating; it didn't mean he didn't have one any more.

'Sorry,' he said.

And he was sorry. If he hadn't been dead, playing man and wife with Toshiko for a couple of nights could have been fun. He was also sorry because he liked Toshiko (strangely he had grown to like her so much more since there had been no chance of – and no point in – bedding her) and he knew that a big part of her was looking forward to their stay here. She had feelings for him that he could never return, and she knew that, but this SkyPoint job was the closest she was ever going to get to playing husband and wife – probably, with anyone.

This was her dream job, he thought. It would have made his stomach turn over, had it still been able to.

He should tell her now, he thought, that this was a mission – that they had a job to do – and anything else going on inside her head was just pure fantasy, and she should quit it right now. The trouble was, he didn't have the heart to do that. How could he do that to a woman that loved him even though he was a walking corpse.

If you loved her, you would.

Christ, he hoped they could clear this business up fast.

The doorbell went.

They looked at each other. They had agreed that Jack and the others should stay away while Owen and Toshiko got settled in at SkyPoint. No one else knew they were there.

'Maybe it's the milkman come to sign us up,' Owen theorised with a frown. He headed for the door. 'What do you like on your cornflakes in a morning?'

He opened the door to a tall woman with cascading blonde hair in a white dress. If she'd had wings coming off her shoulder blades, he'd have believed in angels. Beside her stood an economy copy. Same golden hair, same finely sculpted cheekbones, same blue-green eyes. Just in jeans and a T-shirt with a kitten face on it.

The little girl smiled up at Owen. 'Hello, I'm Alison. What's your name?'

Kids were about as alien as it got for Owen. Some guys couldn't talk to women. He never had a problem there. But kids…

The mother spoke before he had to. 'I'm Wendy, this is Alison. Sorry, my daughter always likes to get in first.'

'What did you do to your hand?'

Alison had noticed Owen's bandaged fingers.

'I had an accident,' he told her.

Behind him, he felt Toshiko come to the door. He felt her hand slip around his waist, the way a wife might squeeze her husband's waist when she found him at the door talking to a cute blonde stranger.

'Hello?' she smiled.

'Wendy Lloyd. This is my daughter Alison. We live just there,' she said, indicating the half-open door across the passageway. Number forty-four.

'Just wanted to welcome you to the block.'

Toshiko leaned forward to shake Wendy's hand.

'Toshiko,' she said. 'And Owen.'

'Hi,' said Owen.

Toshiko looked down at the little girl and tugged playfully on her kitten-face T-shirt. 'I like your kitty cat.'

'Mummy says I can have a real one when I'm six.'

'And how old are you now?' Toshiko asked.

'Five and three-quarters.'

'Not long to wait then,' said Toshiko.

See, thought Owen, that's what he couldn't do – find something to talk about with kids. Largely because all you could talk to them about was kitty cats and puppy dogs and dolls and toy cars. And, quite frankly, he didn't give a shit.

Toshiko straightened up and asked Wendy if she and Alison wanted to come in. Owen, she said, had just put some coffee on. Maybe Wendy caught the look of horror that flashed across Owen's face.

'No, it's all right, you're probably up to your necks in packing cases. I know what it's like on moving-in day. But if you want, why not come over later for dinner? You'll probably be too tired to cook, and we're just sending out for an Indian. You can meet my husband, and I can bring you up to speed on all the SkyPoint gossip.'

Owen was forming a polite decline when Toshiko said they would love to.

Wendy's smile shone, and Owen had another vision of angels.

'Wonderful,' she said. 'Come round about seven and we'll dig out the take-away menu.'

'See you then,' said Toshiko.

And Wendy led Alison away by the hand. The little girl

was still watching them as Wendy closed the door of their apartment behind them.

Toshiko slipped back through their door. 'At least the neighbours seem nice.'

Owen followed her back into the apartment and kicked the door shut with his heel. The Dave Brubeck Quartet had moved on to 'Cassandra'. Maybe that would have chilled out his mum and dad, but right now it didn't do anything for him.

'What are you playing at, Tosh?'

She looked back at him, genuinely puzzled. 'What do you mean?'

'Going around the neighbours for dinner. Look, this isn't for real, you know. Whatever's going on inside your head, Tosh, this isn't us living happily ever after. I'm here to find out what's making people disappear around here, not to fulfil some warped fantasy of yours.'

Toshiko's eyes burned with a moist rage. 'Is that what you think?'

'Oh, come on, Tosh. This is your dream come true.'

'Actually, Owen, no it isn't! This is nothing like my dream come true!'

She couldn't look at him any more. She crossed to the window, stared out across the water and wished she could throw herself into it.

Owen stood still, watching her. He could see her trembling with pent-up rage. He felt like an idiot. How the hell could this be anyone's idea of a dream come true – pretending you were married *to a bloody corpse!*

Still staring out of the window, determined to keep at

least some control of her emotions, Toshiko said, 'I know what we're doing here, Owen. It's my job, too. And that's all I've got, my job.

'But the instruments have drawn a blank. There's not the first sign of Rift activity. And that means the only way we're going to find anything out is from the people that live here. I'm sorry if that means we have to make it look like we love each other, but believe me, Owen, that is no dream-come-true for me. It doesn't even come close.'

Owen stood at the window and looked out over the Bay with her. He wanted to touch her, wanted to tell her that he was a prick, and that he was sorry. But he thought she would tell him to shove it, and he didn't blame her.

Instead he said, 'I suppose we should count that as our first marital.'

TEN

Toshiko didn't want Owen to think a joke was going to get him off the hook just like that.

With barely a word she had gone into the bedroom and grabbed the messenger bag that carried her equipment then told him she was going to take a look around as she went through the front door.

'I'm getting on with the job,' she said as the door closed.

It didn't hit her until she got into the elevator that she was following the ritual of domestic politics she had grown up watching her mother employ on her dad.

Never let a man know you've accepted his apology. Let him sweat a little more first.

Her mother had never actually tutored her in the fine art of male-female power games, but it was the sort of thing she would have said. And the young Toshiko had seen her employ the gambit so many times, she had come to understand its mechanics the way a lion cub learns to hunt.

The longer you leave it, the more opportunity he has to buy you something nice.

Toshiko rode the elevator down to the basement. As long as she was playing sexual politics with Owen, she might as well get on with what she had told him she was doing, she thought. When she and Jack had snuck into SkyPoint before, she had been unable to pick up any Rift activity, but she had been wondering if it was possible that the building itself was somehow masking the energies that would normally mark its presence. She didn't have the first idea how that could be the case, but she figured that the best place to look for a clear trace was at the building's foundation.

So, the basement.

It wasn't part of the regular itinerary for residents using the elevator – access to the basement was through a button with a key that Toshiko guessed would be carried by the building's maintenance people. But it was going to be a pretty special key that stopped Toshiko Sato going where she wanted.

A few seconds later, the elevator doors opened in the SkyPoint basement.

She had pulled up the SkyPoint blueprints in the Hub before Jack and she had made that first visit. She now had them on the screen of her hand-held computer. The basement was below SkyPoint's underground car park, and that put her now at twelve metres below the surface. She shivered. It was cold down here. Nothing all that strange about that, she thought, and the Rift didn't work like so-called psychic activity – supposedly haunted locations were said universally to register markedly lower than ambient temperatures; Toshiko's research had in fact shown that Rift activity often created a slight increase in temperature. Scientifically that made sense: the power involved in tearing a passageway between dimensions would inevitably create an energy fallout that would most easily be manifest as a brief temperature boost. It was basic physics. That was why Toshiko didn't believe in ghosts. Even if there were ghosts, they couldn't hurt you – the things that came through the Cardiff Rift were something else, altogether.

Light from the elevator fell across a board of switches on the wall, but Toshiko took a flashlight from her bag – the darkness of the subterranean level was comforting, it meant that no one else was already down here. If a janitor turned up before she completed her readings, she didn't see why she should advertise her presence.

The flashlight burned a hole in the darkness and picked out an expanse of piping and wiring beyond her. Holding the torch at shoulder height, she stepped into the darkness and the elevator doors hissed to behind her. The only light now was that of the torch beam and the glow of the hand-held. Moving further into the gloom, Toshiko switched screens on the hand-held with a practised movement of her thumb. The SkyPoint plans were replaced by a graphic that would pick up the slightest hint of Rift activity. She had taken four steps across the basement floor and so far the graphics were still. No activity.

As she moved across the basement she swept the flashlight from side to side, and occasionally above her, lighting up the channels of steel ducting that ran across the roof. She had been in places like this before – dark, empty warehouses, derelict hospitals – and, after five years, they were places she knew she would never get used to. The darkness pressed close to you like a living thing and the tiniest sound was magnified inside your head by nervous tension into the most sinister portent of bloody destruction. She had learned to cope with such things, but it was dangerous to ignore them. If nothing else was down here, she knew that Weevils got everywhere. They reckoned that in the city you were never more than a couple of metres from a rat – you could probably say the same about Weevils. Somewhere down here in the vast darkness there would be a manhole cover and under that (and only under that, if she was lucky) somewhere there would be a Weevil.

So Toshiko moved through the darkness, following the tunnel of light ahead of her, every sense testing for danger.

The torch beam settled on a half-open door. What lay beyond it was cast into a darkness that seemed even deeper than that which pressed in around her. Curious, Toshiko moved towards the door. Subliminally, her mind noted the weight of the gun that nestled in the small of her back beneath her leather jacket. A part of her brain rehearsed the motion of dropping the hand-held computer module and yanking the gun from her belt if she needed it.

Gently, she pushed the door open with the toe of her shoe, and she spread the flashlight beam across the room beyond.

The first thing she saw was a half-naked woman.

The brunette wore skin-tight leather trousers that shone like spilled oil, and they were unbuttoned at the waist – like she'd forgotten to do them up, the same way she had forgotten to put anything over her silicon-pumped boobs. She was spread over the bonnet of a sports car and at her feet it said *SEPTEMBER*. Someone – the janitor who used the office – was marking off each day of the month. There was a crude circle drawn around the last Friday of the month. Maybe that was pay day.

Toshiko took in the rest of the room: there was an old table covered in paperwork and old newspapers; there was a kettle and a stained mug. There was a box of tools. And in one corner of the room there was a big, scratched metal cupboard. Toshiko opened the cupboard and saw bottles of what she took to be cleaning chemicals. She closed it again and got down on her hands and knees. The cupboard stood on four metal feet that raised it a little way off the concrete floor. This was what Toshiko was looking for.

From the messenger bag over her shoulder she took a wafer-thin device that was about the size of a cigarette packet. She brought up another screen on the hand-held module and a couple of small diodes flashed into life on the device. She hid it under the cupboard. From there it would relay foundation-level readings to Toshiko's hand-held. There might be no evidence of the Rift down there right now; it didn't mean that was the way things were going to stay.

As she got back to her feet, she heard the noise in the ducting.

Nerves stretched to tripwires, she stood absolutely still, listening to the noise and trying to rationalise it. She found it hard to come up with something that it even sounded *like*.

A little like wind rushing. A little like water spraying. And yet, unmistakeably and somehow horribly, solid.

Something was moving through the ducting overhead.

She glanced at her hand-held module: still no indication of Rift energies.

But whatever was up there was no rat.

And it wasn't human.

Toshiko moved out of the office, her torchlight following the ducting as she traced the progress of whatever was up there.

And then it stopped.

Toshiko stopped with it, her eyes on the metal ducting directly above her. Whatever she and Owen had come to SkyPoint to find, she knew it was just a few feet away, in the ducting above her head.

Why has it stopped? What's it doing?

Suddenly she felt as if she was being watched. As if whatever was up there in the ducting was looking straight through the metal at her, waiting to see what she would do.

Toshiko forced herself to shake off the notion. But she slipped the computer module into the messenger bag and drew the automatic from the small of her back. Then her ears strained for the slightest noise. She heard nothing. She counted the seconds with the beats of her heart. As a minute passed, there was still only silence, and it was as if she had imagined the whole thing.

She ran the torch beam along the ducting. Three metres further on there was what looked like an inspection hatch. She had noticed a stepladder back in the janitor's room. Her stomach turned over: the last thing that Toshiko wanted to do was climb into that steel tube with whatever was up there *waiting for her*. It wasn't just the thought of something unknown, possibly alien and almost certainly dangerous up there. Toshiko wasn't much good in confined spaces. UNIT had made sure of that when they cooped her up for six months in a cell that had been just 1.2 metres square. She knew without any doubt that if Jack hadn't shown up when he did and made her that offer to join Torchwood, then one day the UNIT guard that brought her food would have found her dribbling and crazy in the corner.

But that had been a while back now, and she had coped with a hell of a lot more than being shut in a box. She got the stepladder and set it up beneath the hatch, her ears still straining for the slightest noise from above. She climbed the ladder and wished to God that she had telekinetic powers or a third hand – she was going to need the torch to see by and that meant she had to put the gun away while she opened the catches to the duct. For a moment she thought about getting Owen. Sure, that would be the sensible thing – but she still had a point to make.

She listened again, turning her head a little so that her ear was so close to the metal, so close to whatever was on the other side of it.

She heard nothing.

Quickly, she shoved the gun back into her waistband and snapped open the catches to the inspection hatch. She held the hatch in place against the body of the torch and listened some more as she retrieved the weapon. In her mind she rehearsed what she was going to do next.

Duck. Drop the hatch. Go for it.

Toshiko held her breath. There was still no sound from within the steel duct.

Then she did it like she had rehearsed it.

She moved fast, her muscles beating her synapses – getting it done before she had time to think twice.

The stench hit her even before her head was through the hatch, and she knew what she was going to find in there ahead of the torchlight falling on it.

It was, in fact, only the stench that told her.

What lay along the narrow steel channel, illuminated by the flashlight beam, looked nothing like human remains, but that stink was unmistakeable. More than once she had come across what was left of people that had been savaged by Weevils – they were messy killers but had the good sense to hide what they left behind. Generally, Weevils found a good hiding place and packed it with bodies until there was no room to pack any more. Torchwood would come across a mass grave of Weevil kills on average once every couple of months. But you only had to smell one to remember the stink.

But this was no Weevil kill. Toshiko stood on the stepladder, the flashlight in one hand, her gun in the other and regarded the stinking mess a few feet away from her. She didn't know what had killed this poor bastard – or bastards.

What she saw was a shapeless gelatinous mess that looked mottled and grey in the light of the flashlight, streaked with veins and splotches of red-brown. Here and there, patches of hair clung to it like lichen.

And there was an eye.

Toshiko gasped and almost lost her footing on the stepladder.

The eye stared at her, a large black pupil in a fading blue iris. It had been a beautiful eye once. It was hard to imagine that it had once gazed from anything other than a beautiful face. Now it glinted in her torchlight, set in a mass of decomposing cellular matter.

Toshiko didn't have the first idea what could have done this. She just thanked God that it didn't seem to be around any more. It was time to get Owen. He was the medic; maybe he would have some clue as to what turned human beings into mush like that. She closed the hatch and put the ladder back where she had found it.

She was almost at the elevator doors when Besnik Lucca stepped out of the darkness.

ELEVEN

Owen was angry with himself over what had happened with Toshiko. She was a good friend. When it came down to it she was in fact the only good-looking female he had ever been friends with that he hadn't screwed.

Maybe that was his problem. Owen had known for years that Toshiko wanted to go to bed with him, and for years he had taken an almost perverse delight in denying her. By the time he'd got over that he had actually started to feel too close to her – he hadn't wanted to screw things up between them and almost inevitably that was what sex would have done. But things were different now with Toshiko, he knew.

She loved him.

He had heard her tell him that after Copley's bullet had put a hole in his chest and after Jack used that frigging resurrection glove to bring him back for a few minutes – but before they realised Torchwood was going to be stuck with a walking corpse on the payroll.

I love you.

Not many women had said that to Owen, fewer still that meant it. And none that had known him as well as Toshiko did. Even the woman he had been going to marry hadn't known him that well – after all, that had been a different Owen Harper; that had been before Torchwood.

And maybe that was what got Owen so angry.

Maybe he could have been happy with Toshiko. If he hadn't been dead.

Life was shit. And so was death.

Ten minutes after she left the apartment Owen decided to go and look for her.

He took the elevator. And went up.

The twenty-fourth floor was something special. It wasn't every apartment block that had its own high-rise park. At least, that was how SkyPoint's designers had seen it. They called it SkyPark.

The elevator doors opened onto an open area that had been laid out with plants and trees growing in pots. They hadn't gone so far as carpeting the floor in artificial turf – thank God – but there was a good-sized pond with koi flickering just below the surface. There was even a small kids' play area and what Owen guessed was going to be a coffee stall (he thought they probably wouldn't get the franchise sorted out until the building had rather more residents).

As he stepped out of the elevator he was pretty sure that Toshiko wasn't there. There were a few hidden corners to SkyPark, isolated by walls of potted bushes, but his senses told him straight away that he was alone up there. After all,

all but a few of the building's apartments were still empty, and it was a nice day outside – the odds were all against a busy day on the twenty-fourth floor.

There was always something strange about a park when it was empty, he thought, as he crossed the floor towards one of the benches that had been set to look out across the city below. He guessed it was like any normally busy public place that you came across deserted. It felt eerie and wrong. Like Oxford Street or Times Square in some post-apocalypse movie. He passed through the play area and pushed the small roundabout. It made a quietly oiled sound that was somehow disappointing – he had wanted it to make a sound, to squeal like a banshee or something. Something to add to the surreal feeling of the place.

'It won't go very fast.'

The little voice in the empty park made Owen jump.

He saw the little girl from across the corridor on the thirteenth floor. She was peering at him from behind one of the big tree pots. Owen walked towards her. She was sitting with her back to the pot, a big book balanced on her drawn-up knees.

'Alison. Right?'

'Alison *Lloyd*,' she corrected indignantly.

Owen smiled and wondered if the girl was playing him. He asked her what she was reading. If she told him it was a book, then she was playing him.

'Fairy stories,' she said.

Owen crouched down. Maybe it wouldn't feel quite so strange talking to a kid in a playground if he was kind of the same height. Next to her on the floor was some kind of pixie doll, faded and worn. It looked like the kind of thing that kids sometimes inherited from their parents' old toybox. It looked like it had had a hard life; it had lost one pointed ear and a bright green eye. But the little girl loved it; it looked like she had been reading to it before Owen disturbed her.

'Which fairy story?' he asked.

'Rapunzel,' she told him.

The story of a golden-haired girl locked in a high tower. She didn't seem to see the irony of it. Why would she? Did kids get irony at six, or whatever she had said she was earlier.

'Mr Pickle likes it.'

It looked like Mr Pickle was the doll. Pickle the Pixie. *Why the hell not?*

'Do you play with the other kids up here?' Owen asked, casting a glance around him, wondering where Alison's mother was.

'What other kids?'

'There aren't any other kids living here?'

'Not yet. Mum says there will be one day.'

'Must be a bit lonely.'

Alison shrugged.

'Did you have plenty of friends where you lived before?'

Alison frowned. 'Don't remember.'

See, this is why you don't get on with kids. Always playing bloody games. And what the hell are you doing squatting on the floor with her like this? When her mum shows up what sort of a pervert is she going to take you for?

Owen got to his feet, feeling the child's eyes on him. He couldn't make up his mind if they were suspicious – maybe she already had him down as a perv (kids these days grew up too quick; maybe they had to) – or somehow betrayed, like she didn't want him to go.

'What sort of accident did you have?' she asked.

She was looking at his hand again.

'I shut it in a door,' he lied.

'That was stupid.'

Not so stupid as breaking your own finger to prove a point. That was stupid when you were alive, when a walking corpse did it and the damage was never going to get fixed – now that was *really* stupid!

'Yeah,' he admitted.

'I had an accident,' she said.

'Oh?'

'A car hit me and Mummy, and I died.'

Owen felt oddly like the world had just shifted around him. Not by much, just a couple of disorienting degrees. Just for a moment. He knew the feeling, it had happened to him before. The first time had been when he saw the thing that had been living in his fiancée's head: the alien parasite that had killed her, the thing that had led him to Torchwood. The last time he had felt it had been when Jack had brought him back from the dead and he had realised what he was. It was the feeling that the world was never going to be the same again.

She wasn't dead like him, he understood that. She had been hit by a car and either paramedics had got her heart going again at the scene or she had died for a few seconds later in the operating theatre. Either way, she had been to the same place he had. She had seen the same thing he had, she had *felt* it. And if his tear ducts had worked he would have wept for her. Inside, he cried anyway.

'What happened?' he asked, his voice little more than a whisper, and he found that he was crouched down with her again.

Alison looked at him, and it didn't feel like he was looking into the eyes of a child, yet her voice was without drama, matter-of-fact: 'Do you mean the accident, or after?'

'Oh, there you are! Alison, I've been looking all over the place for you!'

It was her mother. She was crossing the strange twenty-fourth-floor indoor park towards them.

Owen automatically got to his feet and smiled at Wendy Lloyd.

'Hello,' he said.

'Hello again,' she said.

She smiled, but it wasn't quite the same as before, when she had turned up on the doorstep. The smile was pulling against tension. Nothing strange in that, Owen thought: you find your daughter in a lonely park talking to a stranger (and some of the worst strangers can live just over the road from you). What mother wouldn't be a little tense?

'How many times have I told you to stay out of the tunnels, Alison. They're not safe.'

Alison held up the pixie doll like it was his fault. 'Mr Pickle says they're pixie tunnels, and I'll be safe with him.'

Owen was confused. 'Tunnels?'

Wendy shook her head, despairing with her daughter. 'The ventilation ducts. She just loves playing in them. I mean, it's not like they're that big or anything.'

She shifted her look from Owen to Alison as a warning. 'I swear she'll get stuck in there one day, and we'll never get her out.'

She looked back at Owen, annoyed with her daughter but managing a smile. Compared to the dangers out in the big wide world, this they could really handle. 'We keep taping the duct covers up, but she just peels it off and gets through.'

Owen smiled, and looked at Alison. 'I wouldn't worry too much, another six months or so and it probably won't be a problem.'

Alison was going to grow out of her fascination pretty fast.

'If I haven't turned grey by then,' Wendy said.

Alison folded her book under her arm and took her mother's hand. 'I was telling Owen about my accident.'

Owen saw the smile on Wendy's face falter and die and she swung the child up into her arms. It was a protective motion, but Owen wasn't sure that she was protecting Alison from him.

'You know we don't talk about that, Alison,' she said to the child. Then she looked at Owen. 'It's a time in our lives we'd rather forget about.'

She and her husband had nearly lost their little girl – had lost her for however short a period – who wouldn't want to put it behind them? Owen nodded. 'Of course.'

'One reason we moved to SkyPoint,' Wendy said. 'No cars running past the front door.'

'Guess not,' he agreed and looked around him at the area that had been designed for the SkyPoint community to relax in without fear. 'It certainly is quiet.'

'That's the way we like it,' said Wendy, and carried Alison away to the elevator with her.

Owen watched them go, and thought about Rapunzel.

TWELVE

Toshiko had slipped the gun back into her belt just before she reached the elevator in the basement. When Lucca moved out of the darkness there like a phantom she wasn't sure if he had seen it, or if perhaps she should show it to him anyway – business-end first.

She knew who Lucca was; Gwen had pulled the villain's files up in the Hub Boardroom and given them all a rundown on the guy who lived at the top of SkyPoint. There wasn't much likelihood that he had anything to do with what had brought Torchwood to the apartment tower, but he was a nasty complication that Gwen believed Toshiko and Owen would do well to avoid.

So much for that.

Toshiko jumped as Lucca materialised out of the dark, his face lit up like a Halloween mask by her flashlight. He had been lucky, she realised, that she hadn't pulled the gun on instinct and blown his head off there and then. From what Gwen had told her, he wouldn't have been missed.

'You made me jump!' she gasped, at once recognising Lucca and making ready with some kind of story to cover being down there.

Lucca's eyes glittered like diamonds in the torchlight. When he smiled his teeth shone, white and sharp.

The smile didn't make Toshiko feel any more comfortable.

'You're not supposed to be down here,' he said.

'I was just looking for somewhere to smoke,' she said, hoping she got the mix of apology, embarrassment and what's-it-got-to-do-with-you just right. 'My husband doesn't like me lighting up in the apartment.'

'You could have gone outside.'

'And look like one of those sad people that they make hang around doorways these days? No thanks.'

She just hoped he didn't get too close to her. She wouldn't smell of tobacco.

Lucca pulled a pack from his leather jacket and flipped it open with his thumb, then took an unfiltered cigarette from it with his lips the way they did it in old movies. Maybe he thought it would impress her – he looked the type. They were foreign cigarettes – Toshiko thought she could relax on him sniffing out her lie; those things would have destroyed his nasal receptors.

'We're like a couple of kids behind the bike sheds, yes?' he said, and lit the cigarette with a lighter. There was an accent, but it wasn't strong. 'I see you came prepared.'

He was talking about the flashlight.

'Basements are the only place you can go these days. It was the same at our last building. And the locks to keep us out are never really any good. I work in security.' She extended her hand. 'Toshiko Harper.'

Lucca's hand closed around hers like a rattlesnake. 'Besnik Lucca. Your secret is safe with me, Toshiko.'

'If you won't tell anyone, neither will I,' she said and turned towards the elevator, hoping that would signal an end to the conversation. The elevator doors parted at her touch of the button and she stepped into the light of the cabin.

But Lucca came after her, carelessly tossing his cigarette onto the concrete basement floor. His movement was quick and predatory. Toshiko instinctively pressed herself against the elevator's mirrored wall. The doors closed behind him, and Toshiko felt trapped and more frightened than she had been by whatever was in the ducting. She slid one hand behind her back and felt it rest on the grip of the automatic under her jacket.

'Which floor?' he asked.

'Thirteen. Thank you.'

Instead he hit the button for the twenty-fifth. His floor.

'I said thirteen,' Toshiko said, trying to keep the tension out of her voice as she felt the elevator start to climb.

Lucca flashed Toshiko a smile that made her stomach quake. It wasn't some kind of sinister Bond-style villain smile. It was quite the opposite. She had heard Gwen list the crimes that the police had tried but failed to pin on Lucca; he was the kind of man you didn't want to share a lift with. But he was a good-looking man and that smile could make you forget all the bad stuff. That kind of smile could seduce a nun.

'I know,' he said, casually. 'But that was the basement. I thought now you might like to see the view from the roof.'

'The roof?'

'I have the penthouse. There's a roof garden.'

Well, it beat etchings.

'Owen,' she said, apologetically. 'He'll wonder where I am.'

'Your husband.'

'That's – that's right,' she said.

Lucca touched the button for the thirteenth floor, and Toshiko felt the elevator begin to slow. At the same time, she felt his eyes on her. He made sure that she felt them.

'So be it,' he said. 'But you must come. I promise you – up there – it will take your breath away.'

The elevator doors opened on to the thirteenth floor. Lucca moved aside and motioned with an open hand for her to step out. Toshiko released her hold on the pistol behind her back and stepped out into the corridor.

'I'll see you soon, Toshiko,' he said.

The elevator doors closed on him, but somehow it was as if she could still feel him watching her. It felt uncomfortably like the sensation she had experienced in the basement, that the thing in the ducting was watching her. The thought disturbed her.

What disturbed her more was that for a moment – *just a moment,* she told herself – she had nearly gone with him to the twenty-fifth floor.

THIRTEEN

'Basically,' Owen told them, 'it's shit.'

They were in the medical centre of the Hub, Owen's Autopsy Room: Toshiko, Jack, Gwen, Ianto and Owen, looking at a piece of shit.

It was a sample from the SkyPoint ducting.

When Toshiko had returned to the apartment, Owen hadn't been there. He'd turned up a couple of minutes later and said he'd been looking for her.

Toshiko told him about what she had found in the SkyPoint ducting and took him there immediately. She didn't tell him about meeting Besnik Lucca, and she didn't know why. Owen had climbed into the ducting and taken a sample of the foul mess that she had found in there. He had said he could take a fairly educated guess as to what it was, just as Toshiko already had, but he wanted to get back to the Hub to do a proper analysis.

So two hours later they were standing around Owen's sample in the Autopsy Room.

'Something is shitting in the ducting?' said Gwen, raising a single unimpressed eyebrow.

'But not mice,' said Ianto.

Owen had chosen the most stomach-churning sample he could find. It was, after all, Owen. Death had done nothing to leaven his schoolboy delight in putting the others off their dinners. The eyeball stared at them out of the gelatinous chunk Owen had collected in one of the plastic kitchen storage boxes Ianto had included among their moving-in props.

'So spell it out for me, Owen,' Jack said. 'What are we talking about here?'

'It's human cellular matter. It's been broken down. Digested, if you like. If you ask me, whatever did this, this is what it didn't need. The waste product.'

'Shit,' said Ianto, horrified.

'Exactly,' said Owen.

'No. I meant, *shit*.'

'The poor bastard,' said Gwen.

'Bastards,' Owen told her. 'According to my scans there are at least three distinct DNA markers. Three people. Oh. And I found this.'

He produced a small plastic bag. There was something square and metallic inside.

Gwen reached for it and saw that it was a cufflink bearing the picture of a clown.

'Brian Shaw,' she said, flatly.

Jack started to move around the autopsy room. 'OK. So now we know what happens to the people that get taken. What we don't know is, what's doing this and why.'

'Food,' suggested Toshiko. It seemed like the obvious answer.

'I guess,' said Jack. Though there were creatures in the universe that would kill you for other reasons – even procreation. It wasn't too much of a leap to think that there might be things around that would turn a person into a pile of crap for reasons other than eating.

'So, we know it's some sort of creature. These people aren't being torn away by some sort of force created by the Rift. There's something living in SkyPoint and feeding off the residents,' said Gwen.

'SkyPoint is a big place. And it's still largely empty. This creature could be anywhere,' said Toshiko.

'Or any*one*,' Ianto reminded them. 'I'm sure we all remember how much fun a shapeshifter can be.'

He was looking at Gwen. Now that had been the Wedding from Hell. Gwen got bitten by a shapeshifter that passed on its unborn young in its bite. Next morning – the morning of her wedding to Rhys – she was fully pregnant with a baby alien. And then it's shapeshifting mum showed up to rip it out of Gwen – that was Nostrovite childbirth; gas and air wasn't an option.

'This isn't a Nostrovite,' said Jack.

'Thank God,' said Gwen.

'But there are all sorts of shapeshifters,' Owen told them, 'and they're all tricky bastards.'

Jack was musing. 'A shapeshifter that can move through walls and pull people out with them...'

'That's not just shapeshifting, Jack. That's atomic realignment,' Owen told him. 'Changing shape is one trick.

There are all sorts of ways different creatures pull that off, but moving a solid body through brick—'

'You're not telling me it's impossible, Owen. I mean something got at those people and it took them with it the same way it got in. And those apartments may be fitted with every mod-con, but they don't have trap doors.'

'No, Jack. I'm not saying it's impossible. When you get down to an atomic level nothing is solid. Everything is built up of energy particles. Theoretically, it should be possible for other energy particles to pass through. Trouble is, passing the energy particles of a living creature through the energy particles of a brick wall would make driving round Marble Arch blindfold look like a piece of cake. If just one particle touched another, your whole living being would be trapped in the wall.'

'So not impossible, just not very possible?' observed Ianto.

'On top of that,' Owen continued, 'you've got your wall-walking predator that then alters the sub-atomic structure of its victim to get it back through the wall. I said shapeshifters were tricky, but if we've got some sort of wall-walker prowling SkyPoint, then it makes David Copperfield look like my Uncle Bob pulling pennies out of my ears when I was six.'

Jack had listened patiently to Owen's lecture. Now he asked, 'Have you got a better idea?'

Owen shook his head. 'A shapeshifting wall-walker. Shit.'

'Sounds like that's where we came in.' Jack grinned. 'Shapeshifting wall-walker shit.'

But Toshiko wasn't in the mood for jokes. 'That means it could be anyone living at SkyPoint.'

'It also means we can't evacuate the building to deal with this,' said Gwen. 'If what we're after really is one of the residents, then we'd be just letting them out through the front door.'

'Yeah,' said Owen. 'And the neighbours have invited us round for dinner. Better just hope we're not it.'

FOURTEEN

Mr and Mrs Harper went out for dinner that night at just after seven, as they had arranged.

They had got back from the Hub around six-thirty. Owen said he needed a shower. His ability to smell things had been lessened by his no longer being able to breathe, but the receptors in his nose still worked, and his brain was still analysing the signals they picked up, so he was still vaguely aware of the stink of the duct clinging to him. Toshiko said she needed one, too. She took the en suite off the bedroom and Owen made use of the shower in the guest bedroom, warning her not to be long. It had been a long time since Owen had shared an apartment with another woman – not since Katie, the woman he had wanted to marry – but he remembered how long they could take to get ready.

Although they had two bedrooms, they had decided to keep all their clothes in the master bedroom's walk-in closet. A cleaning service for the apartment came as part of the SkyPoint deal and their clothes hanging in separate rooms might have raised eyebrows and possibly suspicions elsewhere in the building. The bed itself was not an issue as Owen wouldn't be sleeping anywhere.

Five minutes later, Owen was showered. Then he remembered that his clothes were across the apartment in the other room. He considered putting on the clothes he had shed onto the bathroom floor – his body no longer sweated and the clothes would have been fine, had he not been crawling around in the building's ducting system a couple of hours earlier. Cursing, he wrapped a towel around his middle and padded towards the master bedroom.

He could hear the shower still running, and slipped quickly through the sliding door into the clothes-lined dressing room.

And found Toshiko in there, naked.

She gasped and pulled the outfit she had been considering across her body.

Owen spun around, putting his back to her. 'Sorry.'

'You could have knocked,' she said.

'I thought you were still in the shower. It's still running.'

'Don't you leave the shower running after you get out, to wash it down?'

'No.'

'I wouldn't want to take a shower at your place, Owen.'

Behind him he could hear the rustle of fabric as naked Toshiko hurriedly got less naked. Trouble was, it was the naked Toshiko that he was going to be seeing all night. And, Christ, what he wouldn't do for an erection right now.

She pressed past him in the doorway. She was wearing a satin blouse that clung to her like a silvery membranous skin and a dark skirt that hugged her shape. He only remembered seeing her in a skirt once before – that had been Gwen's wedding: she had looked good then; she looked good now. Her hair was still wet. He felt an urge to push his fingers through it.

She was looking for a hairbrush among the things that she hadn't yet unpacked – the search helped cover her embarrassment. When she looked up he was still watching her. She thought that he probably didn't realise that he was staring. There were still droplets of water glowing on his skin under the bedroom's recessed halogen lights.

She looked away abruptly.

'Sorry,' Owen repeated, and sounded like a schoolboy caught thinking things he shouldn't have. 'I'll get some clothes.'

And he disappeared into the dressing area, closing the door after him.

Toshiko found the hairbrush and dragged it through her wet hair and thought about Owen standing in her bedroom, wet and all but naked. There hadn't been many men in her bedroom like that. There hadn't been many men, full stop. She had never been particularly good at building that kind of relationship. The lovers in her life could be counted on one hand; just a couple of fingers, if one-night stands didn't count – and she knew that they didn't. That wasn't love, it was just lust, no matter how they tried to dress it up. And lust was OK, it was passionate and it took you some place that was all exploding physical sensation, and you could lose yourself there for a while. But Toshiko wanted love. As she'd looked at Owen standing all but naked in her room, she had tried not to look at the hole that had been blown in his chest by Aaron Copley's gun, but her eyes were drawn to it as inevitably as the droplets of shower water on Owen's shoulders travelled over his biceps and down his arms. The bullet hole was dark, ringed by livid ragged flesh. And as she looked at it she knew that she might probably love Owen until the day she died, but he could never love her.

She realised that she was crying when she heard the dressing-room door open, and she quickly wiped the tears away. She heard Owen clear his throat, uncharacteristically nervous.

'How do I look?' he asked.

Toshiko turned to look at him. 'You look fine.'

'Don't want to let the missus down,' he shrugged and gave her a smile.

Toshiko felt a crack in her heart deepen a little more.

'You won't,' she said, and told him she wouldn't be long.

Owen nodded, hoping they were over the awkwardness, and told her he would be waiting in the lounge.

A few minutes later they were together outside Wendy and Ewan Lloyd's apartment, the secrets of their sham marriage hidden from view.

'Come on in! Come on!'

Wendy had appeared at the door the second time Owen pushed the bell. She had tied back all that blonde hair and was wearing jeans now and a white shirt with the sleeves turned back. She was the kind of woman you could take anywhere dressed like that. Toshiko thought she would probably have made sackcloth look classy. And she wondered if Wendy Lloyd was also a shapeshifting wall-walker that could render you to a pulp of cellular matter.

'Come on,' Wendy said again, as she opened the door wide on the apartment beyond. Toshiko and Owen saw that they weren't the only guests.

'I thought we'd make a party of it,' Wendy explained as she closed the door behind them. 'Seemed like a good opportunity to meet everyone. To welcome you into the SkyPoint family.'

Toshiko exchanged a glance with Owen: if Wendy Lloyd wasn't the creature that came through the SkyPoint walls, chances were that someone here was.

And silk blouses were all very well, but they didn't hide the bulk of an automatic pistol shoved down your skirt waistband too well. She wore a small purse over her shoulder, but that wasn't big enough for a gun, either.

Toshiko regretted her choice of wardrobe. And wished for the gun.

Owen counted twelve people in the apartment lounge. One of them, a balding man with a beer belly came towards them with an extended hand.

'I'm Ewan,' he said. 'Wendy's husband.'

Owen had failed to make the connection and hoped his surprise didn't show. Had he stopped to imagine the kind of man that Wendy was married to, it wouldn't have been the guy pumping Owen's good hand right now.

'Owen Harper,' he said. 'This is my wife, Toshiko.'

Ewan turned towards Toshiko, and beamed, dipping his head. 'Ha Ji Me Ma Shi Te.'

Toshiko smiled, surprised and delighted. 'You speak Japanese?'

Ewan shrugged. '*Speak* is probably a bit of an exaggeration. I worked there for a while.'

'Ewan is an accountant,' explained Wendy. 'And believe me, what they say is completely true. Boring as hell.'

As she spoke she slid an arm around her husband's wide waist. Whatever she said, Owen could see that Wendy Lloyd loved her man, beer gut and all. He also noted that Ewan had orange juice in his hand. Maybe he was cutting down for his wife. Maybe it was three-quarters vodka.

'Get you a drink?' Ewan offered, maybe seeing Owen checking out his own glass.

'Yeah,' said Owen. 'You got a lager?'

'You got it,' Ewan grinned, and shifted to Toshiko.

'White wine spritzer, please,' she said.

'On its way. Wendy will do the introductions.'

And Ewan moved off towards the kitchen as Owen realised the other guests had been closing on them. He resisted the urge to back away, and came up with a smile to share among them.

'Hi. Owen Harper. This is my wife, Toshiko.'

He found that he was getting strangely used to saying that.

For all their hunting-pack circling, the assembled SkyPoint residents seemed to be a pretty friendly, if mixed, bunch. As Ewan had promised, Wendy led the way with the introductions.

Mark and Roslyn Bridges were a middle-aged couple who lived on the eighteenth floor. They were both lawyers who worked for the Welsh Assembly. He was tall and lean with hair that had turned iron grey and probably made him look a few years older than her really was. She was a lot shorter, slightly built, but somehow looked the tougher. She was wearing a black dress right now, but Owen got the feeling that back in their apartment she wore the trousers.

There was a younger couple who lived on the nineteenth and, apparently, right on top of the Bridges. This was Alun Griffiths and his girlfriend Julie Jones. Alun was a photographer who worked in fashion and his girlfriend was a model who – he said – didn't.

'Too short,' Julie explained. 'But who wants to be a clothes horse when you've got bloody melons like these,' she laughed, clutching at them playfully with scarlet-tipped fingers. She laughed like a noisy flushing toilet, and her boyfriend sounded like a busted boiler kicking into life when he joined her. Toshiko caught the look between Mark and Roslyn and got the impression that the soundproofing between floors maybe left something to be desired.

Andrew and Simon Taylor were a gay couple who had moved into SkyPoint after exchanging their civil ceremony vows a few weeks ago and were more delighted than anyone to welcome Toshiko and Owen to the building.

'They'll stop calling us the newlyweds now,' Andrew told them with a smile that was so wide it threatened to dislodge the big red-framed glasses he wore. Andrew and Simon were both writers. Simon wrote travel guides – it was work that took him all over the world, but when it came down to the word-punching he sat back-to-back with his partner overlooking their panoramic Bay view while Andrew worked on the latest in a series of novels featuring his gay Cardiff private eye detective hero and played Bowie loud enough to shake the foundations.

By this time Ewan had delivered Toshiko's spritzer and pressed a glass of lager into Owen's hand.

'Cheers,' said Ewan and raised his glass.

Owen raised his own glass and pretended that something across the room had taken his attention, so that he turned and only wet his lips and didn't actually drink any of the beer. Drinking the beer would not be a good idea, nor would eating any of the food Ewan and Wendy offered. He and Toshiko had earlier agreed that Owen would claim to be a little off-colour and excuse himself from the meal – but with the apartment full of guests it looked like it was going to be easier than expected to get around the problem. When he got the chance he would also put his beer down and by the time everyone else had drunk a few glasses they wouldn't notice that the level of Owen's glass never seemed to fall.

Now they were being introduced to a starched woman who was probably in her thirties but dressed and acted like she was twenty years older. Marion Blake wore her hair in coiled braids that made Owen think of Carrie Fisher in *Star Wars*, only he got the feeling he was never going to see Marion in a bronze-ribbed bikini. He wasn't sure that he would want to. She was skinny, with lips that seemed permanently pinched into a disapproving pout. She looked like the kind of woman who would have lived behind flickering net curtains and filled her nights behind them writing letters of complaint, if she hadn't been living in a tower block. She was PA to the chairman of a Cardiff-based export company, she said. When she moved on, Andrew and Simon told them that from what they had seen of their neighbour, and her frequent visits by the man who had to be her boss, they suspected that her personal assistance extended to more than keeping his diary straight.

Owen was sure the two writers were winding them up, but, hell, he should know better than anyone that things could take on a pretty skewed reality when no one was looking. He glanced at his watch and wondered briefly what time they would get out of there, and how long it would take Toshiko to drift off to sleep afterwards. He had a regular appointment with some pretty skewed reality of his own later tonight and he didn't intend to miss it – and he didn't want Toshiko asking him awkward questions about where he was going, either.

'You probably know everyone in SkyPoint, then,' Toshiko was saying to Andrew and Simon. 'I mean, if you work from the flat. You're probably around more than anyone else.'

'Well, it doesn't take a lot to know everyone,' Simon told her. 'There's hardly anyone else in the place.' He waved at the dozen-or-so people in the apartment. 'The place is like a bloody ghost town in the sky.'

'They built all these apartment buildings in Cardiff and forgot to work out how many people there were that could actually afford to live in them,' said Andrew. 'It's the same right across the city. There are apartment blocks with no more than a handful of people living in them. It's crazy.'

'I heard that some people moved in here, then just took off,' Toshiko said, and sipped her spritzer.

Andrew's eyes narrowed behind their red frames. Owen wondered if it was the kind of suspicious gaze the gay 'tec in his novels gave the killer when they let something slip.

'You're very well informed,' he said with a smile.

'Our lawyer had heard some rumour,' Owen said quickly, though he didn't think Andrew was doing anything more than playing with Toshiko. And he didn't think Andrew was probably the shapeshifting wall-walker, either. He didn't see a creature like that morphing into anything quite as camp as Andrew.

'Well, we heard the same,' he confided, taking a step closer to Toshiko and Owen. 'It's happened twice, apparently. All very mysterious.'

'They probably realised they couldn't afford it and did a moonlight,' Simon offered. 'But Columbo here reckons there's more to it.'

'Oh?' asked Owen, trying to make his interest sound casual.

'It's fiction writers' dementia,' Simon explained. 'They always have to see a story in the simplest of situations.'

Andrew waved his partner's dismissal away with an extravagant motion of his hand. 'And some people are all too happy to swallow what they're given.'

Simon raised an eyebrow and shook his head. 'Sorry, did you just mistake me for Frankie Howerd then, or what?'

Owen saw Wendy having trouble pulling a wine cork and left Toshiko to find out if Andrew actually knew anything useful he could tell them (which he doubted).

'Can I help?' he asked her.

'Oh. Thank you,' she said and passed him the bottle.

Owen suddenly realised he hadn't actually tried to open a bottle of wine since snapping his finger, but he decided he was too deep in now to pull out. Luckily, he managed it OK.

'Alison in bed?' he asked.

Wendy nodded. 'She's not keen on crowds.'

'So, you moved to SkyPoint because of the accident?'

'That's right.'

He could sense already that she didn't want to talk about it.

'Was it really bad?' he asked.

Wendy put the bottle down on the work surface and looked at him. 'Why are you so interested?'

'I'm a doctor,' he said.

'I see. Well, Alison's fine now.'

Owen leaned against the counter and folded his arms as best he could with his busted hand; he was trying to make this look informal. 'It's not Alison I'm so worried about.'

Wendy shook her head, genuinely didn't get it. 'I don't understand.'

'Look, Wendy, I just moved in over the hall today. I don't want to walk in and start telling you how to live your life, or how to run your family.'

'Then don't.'

Trouble was, that was exactly what he was going to do.

'Why don't you talk about Alison's accident?'

Wendy closed her eyes for a couple of seconds, and he wasn't sure if she was reliving the horror of what had happened that day or counting numbers as she tried to control her rage.

When she opened her eyes again she spoke quietly and quickly, like the faster she said it and the less noise she made with the words, the less chance there was of damaging the new life they were trying to make for themselves up here.

'We don't talk about it because two years ago some bastard got into his car after knocking back six pints of lager and ploughed into the side of my car as I picked my daughter up from playschool. I got scratched, but I watched my daughter, covered in blood, die in my arms.'

'But the medics brought her back, Wendy. They saved her life. You've still got her.'

'And I thanked God for that. I got down on my knees in the road, in the middle of the carnage, the twisted metal and the blood, and I cried out to God, and thanked him. I'd been a Christian all my life, Owen. That was how my parents brought me up and I Believed. With a Capital B. But I never prayed to God the way I did that day – while the paramedics worked on my little girl to bring her back; then to thank Him for sparing her.'

Owen looked at her. He didn't speak, he didn't need to ask anything, now he knew what had happened. He just waited for her to tell him.

'But, do you know what, Owen? My life had been a lie. My parents' lives were a lie. They died last year – my mum had cancer, my dad died exactly two weeks later of a broken heart – they died still believing the lie. But I don't know where they went because there is no heaven, and there is no God. Do you know how I know that?'

Wendy tipped the opened wine bottle up into a glass and drank down a couple of gulps.

'Because my daughter told me,' she said.

Owen didn't need to ask what Alison had told her

mother. He knew what lay on the other side of death – real death, the kind that reduced your body to dust. And there was nothing but darkness. There were no long tunnels lit by distant lights, there were no endlessly sunlit gardens where birds sang and loved ones from the past waited, there wasn't even a cloud.

There was just cold darkness. And fear.

Alison had told her mother and she had no option but to believe her. And the lie that kept the human race sane had been exposed.

She didn't refuse to talk about Alison's accident because she was traumatised by the past. She was terrified of the future.

'So now you know,' she said. She flashed him a harsh, humourless smile.

Hope was what kept the world going. Hope that one day you would find somebody you could love and trust, hope that you would never lose them; hope that your team won the cup this year; hope that you found that dream job; hope that you would find the money to pay the mortgage. But most of all, hope that one day – whatever you have told yourself over the years – you will find that life really does go on beyond the deathbed.

'There is no salvation,' she told him. 'This is all there is. I don't mind that so much. You know, I've actually learned to value life more. Every day counts, you don't get it again.'

'There's nothing wrong with seeing life like that,' Owen told her. 'The trouble with God is people think they get a second chance. They don't.'

Wendy drank from her glass. 'If this is all there is, we

should make the most of it? Absolutely. Where's your glass?'

'Oh, I've put it down somewhere.'

'Have another. While you can,' and she started to pour wine into another glass.

Owen hoped that she wouldn't want to toast living life for today, or something.

She didn't. As she poured the wine her eyes misted over again.

'What pisses me off is that my daughter has seen what's waiting for her.'

'She seems to handle it all right. She's happy.'

'Yeah.'

Wendy said it as if that itself scared her a little bit.

'But it's not going to get her again,' she told him with quiet defiance. 'Not for a long, long time.'

She put the wineglass into Owen's hand and moved off across the room. He looked at the drink in his hand and felt the urge to knock it back. Wendy Lloyd was right, her daughter had seen what was waiting for her, and was waiting for all of them in that room – even him, perhaps, one day.

Owen shivered. He hadn't felt cold, or warm, in weeks. Temperature, like pain, meant nothing to him now. He had almost forgotten how it felt. The last time he could remember feeling cold was in the darkness of death, just before Jack had wrenched him out of it with the resurrection glove. That had been a terrible cold, and he felt it again now. Just for a moment.

And Owen remembered that there were worse things

than being undead.

His eyes found Toshiko across the room. She was talking to another couple that Owen hadn't been introduced to. They were both in their thirties, he guessed, and short and fat and dressed as if their invite had read *Hawaiian Theme*; they looked like beachballs on legs. Toshiko was laughing with them. And he wondered if he had ever heard her laugh like that before. He didn't think so. It wasn't that people didn't laugh down in the Hub – Jack was often good for a giggle and Ianto had that dry wit of his, and Gwen knew more dirty jokes than the Blues' locker room had ever heard – but Toshiko usually only smiled and got on with her work. Something was different about her now. Maybe her spritzers were a little heavier on the wine than she normally took them. Maybe she was just more relaxed.

Owen took in the rest of the room. More people had arrived while he'd been talking to Wendy, there were more than twenty people in the apartment now. None of them looked like good candidates for the shapeshifting wall-walker. Maybe relaxing was OK. He certainly liked what it did to Toshiko.

He stayed by the kitchen counter, nursing the wineglass and watched her as a tall black-haired man in a suit approached her. Owen could only see him from the back, but the suit's cut looked expensive and he caught the glitter of a diamond on the man's white shirt cuff as he extended a manicured hand and gently touched her shoulder blade.

Owen felt something stir inside. He knew instantly that it was nothing biological, unless jealousy was a chemical reaction.

Hey, how was that for a headline? *Dead Man Gets Jealous!*

Toshiko turned to look at the man beside her, and Owen saw three things at once: that she was surprised to see him *(because she had expected it be Owen?)*, that she knew the man – and that the man was Besnik Lucca.

He said something to her and Owen saw Toshiko smile.

'Hey, mate. What's happened there?'

Owen saw Alun, the photographer with the girlfriend who had melons that she liked to squeeze, standing beside him. He was looking down at Owen's hand.

The glass had cracked in his grip; red wine was seeping over his hand and down his trousers.

'Shit,' said Owen.

Jealous Dead Man Breaks Glass and Doesn't Notice!

Owen put the glass in the sink.

'Cheap bloody glasses,' said Alun, and he checked the label on the bottle that Wendy had opened. 'Goes with the wine. Still, here, have another one mate.'

Owen had grabbed some kitchen towel and was mopping at the wine stain on his trousers, but his eyes were on Toshiko and Besnik Lucca. The Latvian had managed to draw her away from the beachball couple and was talking to her quietly in a corner. She was looking up at him, smiling.

What was going on here? She knew who Lucca was, she had been there when Gwen ran them through his police profile – maybe she was just playing up to him. This was an undercover job, after all, wasn't it? But that wasn't the problem. It had been the body language when Lucca touched her on the shoulder – and that he had *touched her.*

That meant they had met before.

'So, you're a doctor, Owen,' Alun was saying, he had a glass in each hand now, one for himself and one for Julie Jugs who was dancing by herself over by the window, and making sure everybody saw her – in the apartment, and across Cardiff. 'What do you think?' he asked. 'Reckon she could go up another couple of sizes?'

'Not now, mate,' Owen said and headed across the floor towards Toshiko and Besnik Lucca.

'Tosh?' he said.

She turned to look at him and Owen was sure that he caught something that looked like guilt in her eye. Then it was gone.

'Owen,' she said. 'This is Besnik. He lives in the penthouse. It has a roof garden.'

Lucca turned to meet Owen's gaze. He had dark eyes, almost black. Owen wondered if Alison Lloyd had met Lucca and if, when she looked into his eyes, she was reminded of the same thing that he was.

'I'm pleased to meet you, Owen,' Lucca said to him, offering that same manicured hand that had stroked Toshiko's back. 'You have a very beautiful wife.'

Owen saw Toshiko looking at him over the top of her glass as she sipped. He took Lucca's hand and shook it.

'Thank you.'

'And welcome to SkyPoint. I hope you find what you're looking for.'

'I'm sorry?' said Toshiko. 'What do you mean?'

Lucca smiled. His teeth were perfect, Owen noticed. Crime paid for good dental care.

'Everyone who comes to SkyPoint is looking for more

than just a home,' Lucca said. His voice was warm and exotic, and his black eyes moved around the room as he spoke, touching each of the SkyPoint residents and moving on as he spoke. 'Some are looking for a view, some status, some want a fresh start, some need a place to escape, and some to hide.'

'What about you?' Owen asked.

'I give them what they're looking for. I own SkyPoint. At least, I have a substantial investment.'

'Impressive,' said Toshiko, and Owen tried to make up his mind if she actually meant it. He could tell when she looked at Besnik Lucca that she wasn't thinking about the things Gwen had told them in the Hub.

'So, you're into property?' Owen asked, wondering how many buildings around the city were built on the bones of people that had crossed him. Maybe that was why the cops had never been able to make anything stick: they couldn't afford to tear down half of the new city.

'I have many interests,' Lucca said, his eyes resting on Toshiko, not Owen.

Yeah, extortion, prostitution, robbery, protection, murder…

Owen really wanted to grab Besnik Lucca by the hair and smash his face into Wendy and Ewan Lloyd's steel and plate-glass dining table until something broke. Head or glass, he didn't care which.

Instead, he slid an arm around Toshiko's waist and drew her closer to him then kissed her on the cheek.

'Well, my wife is the only interest I need,' Owen said.

So hands off!

'I'll see you in the lift some time,' Owen told him, and

meant it to sound a little like a threat. He wanted Lucca to get the message. Whether or not he did, Owen couldn't tell. He didn't wait, just guided Toshiko across the room and whispered to her, 'What in the name of god are you playing at?'

FIFTEEN

Things didn't go well for Owen and Toshiko after he escorted her away from Besnik Lucca. She hadn't reacted well to his half-whispered, half-snarled question and as the two of them adopted the positions that couples did when they started arguing at parties – with the minimum of animation and volume, like a couple of wooden figures on a German clock – Owen could still see they were drawing attention from their new neighbours. It crossed his mind that they probably made a pretty convincing married couple – but if they were newlyweds, they probably wouldn't last long.

In the end they made their excuses and took the argument out into the passageway.

'So tell me, what was all that about?' he demanded.

'What?'

'You and Lucca.'

'I don't know what you'rc talking about.'

'Don't lie to me, Tosh.'

And she looked at him, her eyes wide with surprise – and

delight. 'You're jealous.'

He ignored her. 'The man is dangerous.'

He was jealous, and she liked it.

'Maybe I'm attracted to dangerous men,' she said. After all, Owen had always been kind of dangerous. Maybe not the same way as Besnik Lucca, but he had never been a saint. It shocked her a little to think that may have been what got her on to him in the first place.

'Why didn't you tell me that you'd met him before?'

She'd had something like a smile on her face. Owen's obvious jealousy had delighted her. Now his question wiped it off her face as surely as if he'd slapped her. She considered struggling out of his suspicions, faking complete bemusement, telling him he was imagining things. The trouble was, she was a little scared by the fact she had said nothing to him.

'He found me in the basement earlier.'

'Jesus Christ, Tosh!'

'It's all right. I told him I was looking for somewhere to smoke. I lied. He seemed to believe me.'

'And you didn't think it was worth telling me.'

'We're here to find an alien that can move through walls, not an Eastern European crime lord. He's irrelevant.'

'We don't know that. For all we know, he could be what we're looking for.'

Toshiko shook her head. 'No. According to the police profile, Lucca has been living in the UK since 1998. If he was really something that had come through the Rift there's no way he would have stayed off the Torchwood radar this long.'

Owen conceded that she had a point: if he had come through the Rift, Lucca wouldn't be the first with a murderous track record, but he would be the first to set about building a crime empire, never mind a multi-million-pound property portfolio.

All the same, Owen couldn't help worrying about her and, perhaps, for himself. He felt awkward, but he couldn't stop the question slipping out. 'You don't fancy him, do you, Tosh?'

Toshiko glanced aside. She didn't want to look at him when she lied, but the truth was there was something magnetic about Lucca. Something that was unquestionably dark but undeniably sexually exciting. She didn't want to lie, and she found that she didn't need to – she saw the door to their apartment was standing slightly open, and that took over in the priority stakes.

'Owen, look.'

He turned towards the door and she was glad to see that he had brought his gun with him. He pulled it from the small of his back and motioned her to stand back as he pressed himself against the wall of the passageway and edged closer to the open door of their apartment.

There were no sounds from beyond the door, and the only light was the faint orange glow of the Bay lights below.

Owen readied his nerves and bunched his muscles, and sprang through the door, swinging the gun from left to right across the dimly lit apartment. There was no movement, only the wreckage of an inexpert and destructive search.

Toshiko came in behind him, and turned on the lights. The apartment was a mess, someone had gone through it like a tornado that had up-ended furniture, torn out drawers and spread their contents across the floor and, in the bedroom, slashed the mattress.

'So much for SkyPoint security,' breathed Toshiko.

But she knew this was no burglary. This was a warning.

'I'd say someone was on to us,' Owen observed casually as he put straight an up-lighter. 'I'll give you three guesses.'

Toshiko went into the dressing room. She had hidden her gun and the hand-held computer module on top of one of the wardrobe units. But whoever had turned over the flat had been as thorough as they had disorderly.

'My gun has gone,' she told him. 'And my monitor.'

Owen tossed her the phone from beside the bed. 'Did he give you his number? Maybe you could ask for them back.'

Toshiko threw the phone onto the bed, angry.

'This doesn't make any sense,' she said. 'We're not the police, we're not interested in Besnik Lucca.'

'But he doesn't know that. All he knows is that we're after something.'

'I hope you find what you're looking for.'

'Exactly.'

'The bastard.'

'Now we're making progress.'

Owen had put his gun down on the bed. Toshiko grabbed it, checked it, and shoved it in the waistband of her skirt. She didn't care if it ruined the line of her blouse now.

Owen got to his feet. 'And where do you think you're going?'

'He's got my equipment. I want it back.'

'No, Tosh. Give me the gun.'

Toshiko glared at him. 'I've held my own against all kinds of aliens, what makes you think I can't handle Besnik Lucca?'

Owen regarded her carefully. 'He's a man.'

Toshiko felt anger course like electricity through her, setting every nerve in her body alight. 'Screw you, Owen.'

She turned and left the bedroom, headed for the front door.

Owen cursed himself, and went after her. 'Tosh! I'm sorry – wait!'

But she was already going through the door. She slammed it shut without even looking back.

Owen shook his head, frustrated and angry with himself. The second time today he had acted like a prick. Nothing new there, he'd done it pretty much all of his life. Difference was, this time it was sending Toshiko into big trouble.

Still, he'd catch her before she got to the lift.

He reached for the door handle. It wouldn't turn.

What?

It wasn't that it was locked. If it had been locked, the handle would have turned, but the bolt wouldn't move. But the handle was jammed solid.

He yelled her name, and tugged on the door – but if she heard him she didn't reply and the door didn't move. Like the door handle, it was jammed unnaturally solid.

Owen backed away from the door. Instinctively, he knew that something was wrong here – *very wrong*.

And the thing that melted out of the wall and came for him proved it.

SIXTEEN

Toshiko rode the elevator to the twenty-fifth floor with the gun in her hand. She decided there was no point in a pantomime; Lucca knew that she and Owen were not what they claimed to be, and he knew that they had weapons. The fact that she still carried a gun, despite his goons' search-and-retrieve operation in their apartment, might help limit the discussion and get her what she wanted – and out of there again – faster.

She had gone back to the Lloyds' party first, looking for Lucca and ready to coax him out of there and confront him. Lucca had already gone. But Toshiko was in no mood to let him get away. She didn't stop to think about Owen's concerns for her; she was still running on the pulse energy of anger. She was angry with Owen, and just as angry with herself. There was something to prove here – damn it, there was a *lot* to prove here. To herself, as much as Owen.

Was she really so pathetic that she could face off against horrible things from far-off galaxies, but she just couldn't hack it when it came to men? With her scientist's head in gear she had to admit that the empirical data was not in her favour.

Screw that!

This was where things changed.

She felt the elevator settle on the twenty-fifth floor. She waited for the doors to open. They didn't. Instead she heard Besnik Lucca's voice. She almost jumped, it sounded as if he was in there with her.

'Toshiko. I knew you would come. But, please, put your weapon on the floor.'

Toshiko scanned the elevator cabin. There was a camera. There had to be. She saw her own reflection in one of the mirrors, the gun looked big and heavy in her hand.

'Please,' Lucca coaxed. 'Then we can talk.'

'We're not police,' she called out. 'We're not interested in you, Lucca. We're no threat to you.'

'My angel, anyone who carries a gun to my door is a threat. Put it on the floor.'

Toshiko did as she was told.

'Now step back against the wall, and stay there.'

She took a step backwards and felt the cold glass of the mirror on her back through the thin silk that she wore.

The elevator doors parted, revealing two men who looked part-gorilla. One held a gun on her, the other collected the weapon on the floor, then gestured for her to step out.

The apartment was huge, tastefully furnished and decorated with artwork that she knew was both expensive and original.

The two goons left her to wander across its white carpet

unhindered. She followed the slight breeze that moved through the apartment and found Lucca standing in the roof garden waiting for her.

It was a warm September night, and he had lost the jacket to his black suit. He stood on the terrace watching her approach, and he was smoking one of the same foreign cigarettes she had seen him with before.

The garden was lit with subtle lighting, and he had been quite right: even at night, it was breathtaking.

He stood next to a table that was lit by lights in the floor. There was a champagne bottle cooling and a couple of glasses. She got the sense that he had known she was coming, maybe before even she had.

'I see that you chose not to bring your husband,' he said.

'You know he's not my husband.'

'Which simplifies matters a great deal,' he said, and poured the champagne.

'I didn't come here to drink champagne with you.'

'That's a shame. We had seemed to be getting along so well.' He sipped from one of the glasses. 'And the champagne is at the perfect temperature.'

He held a glass out to her. Toshiko ignored it.

'We're not interested in you,' she told him again.

'We?' he asked, placing the glass back on the table. 'And just who are *we*?'

'Torchwood.'

He looked at her blankly. 'I'm sorry. It means nothing to me.'

'There is something in this building, Mr Lucca, that is killing people.'

Lucca laughed, and threw himself carelessly into one of the big chairs out on the terrace. 'I take it that you mean, apart from me.'

'We know all about you, Lucca. But we're not interested. You're not the kind of scum we have the licence for. Or the stomach.'

He leaned forward, intent. 'So what exactly is it that we're talking about? A life form of some kind that can pass through walls and takes people with it, just sucks them back out through the wall, as if they had never been there?'

Toshiko felt her body charge with nervous excitement. 'Yes. Exactly. Have you seen it?'

Lucca smiled a little. 'I see everything.'

He had a remote control in his hand. He pressed a button and a panel in the garden lit up. Lucca had a TV in his garden, as well as in his shower.

The garden TV didn't particularly shock Toshiko. Anyone who lived half a mile up in the sky and still needed a lawn sprinkler was going to be a little on the flash side. What shocked her was what she saw on the screen.

'I think you missed a bit, just there,' he said, pointing to the back of his own neck.

On screen, Toshiko was showering.

'You pervert,' she growled.

Lucca chuckled. 'A little perversion, a little paranoia… I built this place as my fortress. I have a great many enemies. But up here no one can reach me. From here, if I need to, I can control the elevators, the fire doors, the air-con. Everything. And I see everything.'

He toggled the remote and the image on the screen

changed: it was Owen crossing the apartment earlier that night with the towel wrapped around his waist. Lucca froze the frame. The hole in Owen's chest was clearly visible.

'I see everything,' he said. 'I just don't pretend to understand it all.'

'All we want to do is to stop this thing killing people. You're in as much danger as anyone. Let us deal with it.'

Lucca looked at her for a long time, as if he were considering, or perhaps just playing games.

In the end he said, 'No.'

And the two men that had been waiting for her outside the elevator grabbed Toshiko from behind.

SEVENTEEN

Owen was surrounded by darkness. It was complete and total, and he knew that it was Death.

He had been here before. He remembered it the way that young babies must remember the womb.

There was a strange sensation of suspension. Like floating in the densely salted water of a relaxation chamber. Except that there was little that was relaxing about Death. It was cold, and every nerve in his body was screaming with tension. Because although this was Death, and this was the end, with no afterlife, with no hope of resurrection or salvation, he knew – as all the dead knew – they were not alone here.

There was something in the darkness.

And, whatever it was, it would find him defenceless because he could not move, he could not run and there was nowhere to hide. The darkness may have been total but instinctively he knew that *it* could see him.

Owen!

And sooner or later it would come for him.

Owen!

Just as the thing had come for him out of the wall.

Owen!

And shook his shoulder.

'Owen!'

Consciousness hit him like a hammer right between the eyes.

'Jesus Christ!' he gasped.

'Owen, are you all right?'

This time it was a different voice. A woman's voice. He found himself on the carpet in the SkyPoint apartment. Gwen and Jack were crouched over him.

Jack was smiling. 'Thought we'd lost you again there, buddy,' he said and shook Owen's shoulder once more.

'It's difficult to tell with a corpse,' said another voice.

Owen turned his head and saw Ianto over by the sound system. He really hoped Ianto hadn't been going through the CD collection in case he had passed on for keeps this time.

'Yeah, well I was waiting for someone to give me the kiss of life, wasn't I?' he said, looking at Gwen.

'So what happened?' Jack asked, taking in the apartment and throwing himself onto its oversized couch. 'You missed your ten o'clock call-in. We got round here and found you on the floor.'

Gwen was helping Owen to his feet as his head caught up with him.

'And where's Tosh?' she asked.

'Lucca,' Owen gasped. His memory falling back into place

with the impact of a bomb. Quickly he brought them up to speed with what had happened up to Toshiko slamming the door on him.

'Then it came out of the wall,' he said.

Somehow it had seized the door so that he couldn't escape, and then it had come for him. Emerging from the wall, a shapeless mass that was neither solid nor gas, or liquid. Like nothing he had ever seen before. But there had been lights within it, like stars. It had been like looking into a galaxy that came drifting towards him, enveloping him.

... That was all he could remember.

'But it didn't take you like it did the others,' observed Ianto.

'Maybe it prefers fresh meat,' said Owen.

'We don't have time to work it out now,' Gwen told them. 'This creature – whatever it is – is going to have to wait. First we have to get Tosh back from Lucca.'

Jack leaped over the back of the couch. 'That's right. Come on.'

As one, they moved out into the passageway, but they hadn't reached the elevator when a man came crashing through the stairwell doors. He was in his pyjamas, a dressing gown flapping around him. It was the beachball man from the Lloyds' welcome party, his face was pale but his eyes were red with tears. All he could do was cry one word again and again...

'Gillian! Gillian!'

Gwen caught him in her arms. 'Calm down, love. Calm down. What is it? What's happened?'

'She's gone,' he cried. 'She's gone!'

Behind them, another door opened. It was Andrew and Simon, disturbed by the beachball man's cries.

'What on Earth's going on?' Andrew demanded.

But Simon saw his distressed neighbour. 'Ryan? Whatever's wrong?'

Ryan the Beachball's eyes were huge, threatening to burst out of his head. 'Something, it took her! Gillian! It came out of the wall!'

Andrew raised his eyebrows in disbelief and looked at his partner. 'I never took him as one for the…' And he mimed a spliff.

Owen turned towards them. 'He isn't. He's not hallucinating. There's something in the building and everyone in it is in danger. You were right before, Andrew, people haven't been running out on their payments. People are getting killed. So do yourselves a favour, pack a bag and get out.'

'You're joking, aren't you?' said Simon. 'This is some sort of a wind-up.'

'No,' said Jack. 'It isn't.'

Above him on the wall was the fire alarm. He pulled his Webley from its holster and used its butt to smash the glass. The building was instantly filled with the scream of an alarm.

'OK,' he said. 'Let's get everybody out of here.'

'I thought we'd said we couldn't evacuate the building,' Ianto pointed out, 'in case we lost the shapeshifter.'

'That's right,' said Jack. 'But on the other hand, look at the size of this place. We could be here months and never find it.'

'I don't follow,' said Gwen shaking her head.

'I do,' said Owen. 'This is its hunting ground. We reduce the food supply.'

Jack grinned. 'Exactly. With the residents gone there's just us.'

He looked pretty pleased with his plan; the others looked at each other. They would become the hunters and the hunted. It made sense. The only problem was that from the way Owen had described what attacked him, it didn't sound like bullets were going to have a whole lot of impact.

But that was going to have to wait now; there were people showing up from their apartments. Owen saw Wendy and Ewan Lloyd running towards them. They had hurriedly dressed and had Alison between them in her dressing gown. She held Wendy's hand with one hand, the other clutched the pixie doll to her chest, intent on saving her own most treasured possession.

'What's going on?' Ewan demanded, looking flushed with barely controlled panic.

He was looking at Owen, but Jack answered. 'There's an emergency. You have to get out now.'

'Is it a fire?' Alison gasped, her eyes large with excitement.

Owen bent down to her. 'No. It's not a fire, but you have to get out of the building as quickly as you can. Don't worry, you'll be safe.'

'If it's not a fire, what's happening?' demanded Wendy. 'And who are you people?'

'Everything is going to be fine,' Gwen told her. 'Just get into the lift and leave the building.'

As she spoke, she was easing the family towards the elevator.

'No,' Ewan said, suddenly defiant. 'Not the lift. Not if there might be a fire. It's dangerous. We'll take the stairs. Come on, Wendy.'

'There isn't a fire, Ewan,' Owen said quickly. 'The lift's quicker.'

'We're not using the lift!' he snapped.

The elevator doors opened, and Andrew and Simon went for it without a second thought, taking the whimpering beachball man with them.

'Well, we are,' said Andrew. He lashed an accusing look at Simon. 'I always told you there was something wrong with this place, but you wouldn't listen, would you?'

Ewan was drawing his family towards the stairs. 'Come on, Wendy, Alison. This way.'

Owen strode after them. 'OK, if you want to take the stairs, I'm coming with you.'

Ewan glared at him. No way did he want Owen with them, but right now he didn't seem to have any choice. Owen didn't stop to think about it. If Ewan wanted to be an arse, that was up to him.

As they went through the doors to the stairwell, Owen turned back. 'Make sure you get Tosh, Jack.'

'Don't worry,' Gwen told him.

And Owen was gone.

Jack turned to Ianto and told him to take the elevator down to the ground floor with Andrew, Simon and the beachball man. 'Pull up the records on the desk computer in the reception hall – there's got to be a list of everyone who lives here. Check them off as people reach the ground. I want to know that everybody is clear.'

Ianto nodded and jumped into the elevator cabin. Andrew glanced at him appreciatively, then caught Simon's look. Ianto just hoped it was a very fast ride to the ground.

He saw Jack wink at him as the door closed on the elevator cabin and it began to descend.

At the same time Jack checked the cylinder of the Webley .38. All six chambers were loaded.

'OK,' he said to Gwen. 'Item One – let's get Tosh back.'

Gwen pulled her own automatic out.

And then the fire alarm stopped. And the lights went out.

EIGHTEEN

The sudden silence was deafening; the darkness, blinding.

Jack and Gwen threw themselves against the walls. It was an instinctive reaction. Made them a harder target. It was only a half-second later that they both realised that this time, in this building, the walls might not be such a good place to go for cover. They looked at each other from opposite sides of the dark passageway as their eyes grew accustomed to the night light that fell through a window further along.

'Maybe not,' said Jack.

Together they stepped away from the walls and went back-to-back, their eyes searching the darkness.

'What happened?' Gwen whispered.

'At a guess, we just lost power.'

As he spoke, emergency strip-lights at the bottom of the walls started to flicker into life, giving the passageway a muted green illumination.

'Yeuch,' said Jack. It sounded like he'd just stepped in something.

'What?' Gwen hissed.

'I do not look good in green.'

'Jack?' It was Ianto's voice in his ear. 'What's going on?'

'Where are you, Ianto?'

In the elevator cabin, Ianto ran his eyes down the string of floor numbers.

When the power had gone the lift had lurched to a stop and for a few seconds they had been plunged into total darkness. Andrew had squealed with fright, and Simon told him to grow up. Then a small emergency light had come to life on the ceiling, so Ianto could make out the numbers.

'I think we're between the sixth and seventh floors,' he said at length. 'That's just a guess.'

'Everybody OK?' asked Jack.

Ianto looked at his cabin mates. Andrew's eyes behind his red frames looked like they'd been drawn by Chuck Jones, but he was OK. Simon had an arm around the silently heaving shoulders of the fat man that he occasionally called Ryan. The fat man was the only one Ianto worried about: he was already stressed, having seen his wife get pulled through the wall, now he was trapped in a lift between floors. He could have a heart attack. Or he could turn crazy.

'So far, so good,' he told Jack.

'Sing a few campfire songs. We'll get to you soon as we can.'

Jack turned to Gwen, she had taken a hand-held module from her jacket pocket and was running quickly through screens.

'What have you got?' hc asked.

'The SkyPoint blueprints. Besnik Lucca has the whole of the twenty-fifth floor, penthouse suite, roof garden…'

'Has he got a jacuzzi? I bet he's got a jacuzzi. Maybe if we get this sorted in double-time…'

'Doesn't say anything about a jacuzzi. What it does say is there's no way up there other than the lifts.'

Jack wiped his mouth with the back of his gun hand, feeling the humour drain out of him. 'So we can't reach Tosh while the power's down and, you know, that gives me a really bad feeling about what's going on here.'

Jack spoke into his comms again. 'Owen. Are you there?'

Owen and Toshiko had decided not to wear their comms while they'd been playing Mr and Mrs in case someone had noticed them, but he had taken the earpiece from his pocket when the lights went out. He was there when Jack called him.

'Here, Jack.'

He was two floors below with the Lloyds. And Ewan had a broken ankle. When the power went they had been hurtling down the concrete steps, in the sudden darkness Ewan had lost his footing and gone down heavily. The emergency lighting on the stairs wasn't up to a glow-worm's arse, and together they had managed to help Ewan into the passageway on the eleventh floor, where Owen had quickly examined the injury. There was no way Ewan was going to make it down another twenty turns of the staircase down to the ground.

He told Jack all of this quickly, uncomfortably conscious that Ewan was sitting on the passageway floor with his back against the wall, and that Wendy and Alison were crouched around him. Owen's eyes flickered from one wall to another. The spacious hallway of the eleventh floor had become strangely and insidiously claustrophobic.

He missed the comforting weight of the automatic in his hand. He wasn't sure how much good it would be against something that could slip through the atomic structure of a brick wall, but it would have felt good anyway.

'Listen, Owen, I think Lucca has cut the power. It puts the elevators out of commission and that makes him unreachable.'

'And traps us with whatever that thing is,' said Owen.

'Maybe he's hoping it will do his work for him,' Gwen suggested.

'In the old days in Eastern Europe there were noblemen who gave their enemies a sporting start, then set their hunting dogs on them. But this is the twenty-first century, and I have something that comes through the walls.'

Jack, Gwen, Owen and Ianto all froze. Besnik Lucca had whispered into their ears.

Above them, on the twenty-fifth floor, he stood in the monitor room that showed him the Torchwood team on three different screens, and spoke into the communications device he had found in Toshiko's purse.

Jack hated the sound of the man in his ear, he felt contaminated by it. Biting down on his anger because he didn't want to give Lucca the satisfaction of knowing he had got to him, he said, 'What have you done with our friend?'

Lucca moved unhurriedly away from the monitors and into the lounge. He had Toshiko gagged there, tied to the arms of an armchair, but unhurt.

'She's a little tied up right now, but otherwise well,' Lucca said.

'What do you want, you bastard?' Owen demanded.

Toshiko's eyes followed Lucca around the room as he ambled through it, taking in the treasures of his art collection. Unlike the rest of SkyPoint, the penthouse remained drenched in light – it was clearly fed by a separate power supply.

'I have a proposal for you, Torchwood. I have no real idea who you are, or who you represent, but I have had the fortune to study some of your equipment and your methods. You are clearly well resourced and also resourceful.'

'Thanks for the compliments, Lucca,' Jack scowled, 'but I'd rather you got to the point.'

'An Englishman's home is his castle, don't they say, Jack? I presume the dictum still stands in Wales. Perhaps not, as the English built their castles here to subjugate the natives.

'Well, SkyPoint is my castle, my fortress. As perhaps you can imagine, a man in my position has many enemies – those from my homeland that are still looking for me – people here that would take from me what I have worked for.'

'Don't you mean stolen and killed for?' said Gwen.

Lucca ignored her. 'My castle has many fortifications but they are, as yet, untested. I have every reason to believe that they cannot be breached, but only the determination of a skilled and motivated force can prove that.'

Jack shook his head in disbelief. 'You want us to prove your security systems? Take a hike, Lucca.'

'If you can get to her, Toshiko will be waiting for you, unharmed and free to go.'

'And if we don't?' barked Owen.

Lucca shrugged. 'That won't concern you. Because you will be dead.'

Jack looked at Gwen. He didn't want to play Lucca's game, and he sure as hell didn't care for his rulebook, but he didn't see what kind of an option they had.

'At least put the power back on so that we can get the residents out of the building, Lucca. They don't have to be a part of this, and there's still something alien here that's killing them.'

In his apartment, Lucca shook his head with a sick smile. 'And if I restore power you have a twenty-second elevator ride to my front door. I doubt that you would get through it, but it would compromise the standards of our experiment. Everyone stays in the building. And, incidentally, you will find that the fire doors and stairwell doors are also locked.'

Gwen lurched towards the doors that led to the concrete emergency steps. They rattled noisily, but wouldn't budge.

Jack boiled inside. 'And what makes you think this thing that's in here with us won't come and get you?'

Lucca had found his way back into the monitor room now. He watched Jack on the screen. There was no anger in the man's voice, but as he stood there in that long coat of his, unaware so far that Lucca could see him, there was no disguising the fury he felt in his body.

'You're clearly not a gambling man, Jack.'

'I don't know, I've played some pretty high stakes in the past.'

'Then you should understand. I'm gambling that you are as good as you think you are. Just that you're not as good as me.'

Jack found that the smile came to his lips easily. 'Oh I'm good, Lucca. I'm very good.'

Lucca's voice came back to him: 'Then I have no need to wish you luck.'

NINETEEN

Lucca had finished talking. Owen could hear that the line had gone dead. There was no point in checking back in with Jack, with Lucca plugged into the comms circuit that would only be stupid. And Owen's priority hadn't changed. He knew that Jack would work out some way of getting to the twenty-fifth floor and rescuing Toshiko – what he had to do was get Alison and her parents out of there.

It didn't sound like the elevators would be powering up again any time soon, so that only left the stairs. Lucca may have thought he'd secured them, but Owen knew plenty of ways of getting through a locked door. He also had to get Ewan's ankle strapped up and find him some sort of crutch to help him down the steps. All of which meant he was going to have to get through another door first, and into one of the apartments.

The trouble was, SkyPoint's door designs had moved on a long way from the kind you could just shoulder in, and these days Owen wasn't at all sure if his bones were going to be up to the job. A busted hand he could probably live with – if that was what you wanted to call it – a shattered shoulder that would also put his arm permanently out of commission was another matter entirely.

Instead he decided to think laterally.

He decided to hammer on the apartment doors and see if anyone was still home. He'd seen *The Towering Inferno*, and there had been no end of people that missed the fire alarms going off. Sure, Robert Wagner had died with a wet towel on his head, but who was going to take that as a salutary lesson in high-rise fire survival? People ignored fire alarms in hotels all the time. You generally called them stupid, and dead. But it happened.

He got an answer at the third door he tried.

It took him a few seconds to recognise Marion Blake. If ever there had been a shapeshifter among the guests at the party that night, it looked like it was her. The Carrie Fisher braids had gone and she now wore her hair in a single dark ponytail that she wore cast over her shoulder and trailing over the latex bustier that she wore with fishnet stockings. The pinched, disapproving expression had gone. Her lips were painted a glistening red. And in her hand she had a coiled whip.

She was as shocked to see Owen, as he was her. And tried to slam the door in his face. Owen didn't think his luck was going to hold out for a second apartment and risked his shoulder against the door.

'Look, I'm sorry but this is kind of an emergency,' he said.

Marion looked out at him, and beyond him to Wendy

and Alison and Ewan, who had by now turned pale with the pain of his injury.

'I was going to a fancy-dress party,' said Marion.

It was now around one o'clock in the morning. Even if it had been true, it didn't improve the situation.

'Ewan's hurt, and we have to get out of here,' said Owen, as he pushed the door open and helped Alison's father into the apartment. 'Didn't you hear the alarm?'

'It stopped so quickly, I just thought it was an accident,' she said. Then gave the Lloyds a brazen smile. 'What an unexpected pleasure.'

Owen got Ewan onto Marion's couch and started to look for something he could use as a splint. His eye settled on the coiled whip that she had forgotten she still held. Owen grabbed it from her. The leather-bound handle was perfect.

'Have you got another one of these?'

She looked at him with horror. 'What? Why would I have another—'

Owen didn't have time to tango towards the truth with Marion. That was no fancy-dress costume she was wearing. And the whip was no fun-shop toy. Either Marion Blake was seriously into S&M or she had been waiting for a paying client – and either way, Owen was pretty sure she'd have another whip close at hand.

'Just get it,' he said.

As he expected, she went through into the bedroom.

Alison bent her head to the pixie doll and seemed to listen to it for a moment, then turned and looked at her mother. 'Mr Pickle says, does Miss Blake work in the circus?'

Wendy couldn't help bursting into laughter, and Owen joined her, enjoying the release. Ewan didn't laugh, he was pale and sweating.

'I need to go to the bathroom,' he said. 'I'm going to be sick.'

'It's all right, hold on. I'll find you a bucket or something,' said Owen.

But Ewan swung his legs off the couch, grimacing and defiant. 'No,' he said. *'I want to go to the bathroom.'*

Owen gave an *if it's that important to you, mate. Just don't puke down me on the way. I've got enough problems* shrug.

Ewan put his arm around Owen's shoulders and together they shuffled towards the bathroom. Owen left him to it in there, wondering if Alison's dad really did feel sick or if he was just too embarrassed to admit that he was crapping himself.

Another advantage of being dead, Owen noted. No matter how bad things got these days, the fear of crapping himself (which could be considered a professional hazard working for Torchwood) no longer applied.

As Owen returned to the lounge, Marion emerged from the bedroom. She had wrapped a dressing gown over her latex and fishnets. It was silk, not the towelling number he would have expected the woman he had met earlier to wear. The more he saw of Marion Blake, the more certain he was that her position as PA to some captain of Cardiff industry was no more substantial than the stockings she wore right now. And she had brought him the other whip.

Owen told her to leave it with the other one and asked her about the kind of household cleaners she kept.

'Oh, God. I hope Ewan's not making a mess in there,' she gasped.

Owen had already made his way into the kitchen area and was going through her cupboards. 'Even if he is, Marion, I'm not cleaning up after him.'

He found a bottle of liquid drain-cleaner and brandished it triumphantly. 'Good start.'

Wendy had put her hands protectively on her daughter's shoulders. 'Do you want to tell us what you're doing?'

Owen found another couple of bottles and started to scan the chemicals listed on their labels. 'The only way out of here right now is down the stairs, and Count Dickula on the top floor has locked the doors. But that doesn't mean we can't get out.'

Wendy was incredulous. 'You mean you're going to blow the doors open?'

Owen nodded. 'The average kitchen has everything you need.'

He saw her draw Alison a little closer, a little further away from him. 'Just what sort of a doctor are you?'

'The sort you can trust,' he said, and fixed her with his eyes. He saw her think about it hard, and saw the slightest movement of her head.

Yes, she thought she could trust him. Owen only hoped she was right and yanked open one of Marion's kitchen drawers, found a spoon and started to measure out the cleaning chemicals.

Two floors above, Jack was looking at the SkyPoint plans on Gwen's hand-held module. There was nothing in them to suggest the defences that Lucca had alluded to, but whatever they were he didn't suppose they were the kind of thing that got registered with the City Council. All they seemed to confirm was bad news: that there was no way up to Lucca's apartment other than by the elevator.

'So Lucca is in control of the power and the elevators,' he said.

'And, it's reasonable to assume, everything else,' Gwen confirmed.

'But he's taken control. Those things have to be run from somewhere else under normal circumstances.'

The small computer unit in Gwen's hand cast a bluish light over her face as she scrolled through the pages. She found what she was looking for – there was a control room down in the basement.

Jack grinned. 'Then maybe we can just take control back again. Override his override.'

Gwen nodded without enthusiasm. 'Maybe we could. If we had Tosh. I know you're a man of hidden talents, Jack, but I never see you getting hands-on with the computers in the Hub.'

Truth was, where he came from computer science was a little more advanced than they even had in the Hub, and who needed to know how a light switch worked so long as you could see where you were going when you pressed it? Jack was more of a physical player than a tech. Like Gwen.

Which meant that if they were going to rescue Toshiko they were going to have to do it with muscle, not technology.

'What about the exterior?' he said.

'So you're Spider-Man now, are you?'

'I'm thinking laterally.'

She shook her head. 'Jack, Lucca's apartment is over sixty metres up.'

'And it has a roof garden. Show me the plans.'

She did as she was told. Jack took the module and zoomed in and around the 3-D plans of the highest part of the building.

And he saw what he was looking for.

'Jack, you're crazy,' Gwen said.

'It's the only way.'

She bit her lip, knowing he was right. If there was any flaw in Lucca's fortress defences, the chances were that Jack had just found it. There were just two problems.

One: It was probably impossible.

Two: They'd have to get to the twenty-fourth floor first.

'So what are we waiting for?' asked Jack.

He walked across to the locked doors to the stairwell, and turned to Gwen. 'You do have the key, don't you?'

He stepped back as Gwen raised her weapon, nesting her gun grip in the palm of her left hand, and took aim.

The sidearm was a specially developed variant on the Glock 20, modified to carry a double-clip of thirty 10mm rounds with a machine-pistol mechanism that could fire the full load in under ten seconds. Gwen fired the whole double clip into the door in less time than it took the average man to die from a single bullet. The sound was deafening and the air smelled of cordite. The door panel was perforated by a circle of bullet holes.

As Gwen ejected the spent clips and replaced them, Jack

stepped forward and kicked at the weakened body of the door. A few seconds later there was a hole big enough for the two of them to step through and they started to make their way up the steps.

Several floors below, Ianto and his companions in the elevator had made themselves as comfortable as they could on the floor. According to the acrylic plaque on the wall of the cabin, it was supposed to carry no more than ten people at a time. Ianto thanked God that they hadn't been travelling at maximum capacity when the power went. It already felt like they were running out of oxygen. He knew that was ridiculous, the cabin wasn't airtight; they weren't going to suffocate, it was just getting hot, that was all. He had already peeled off his jacket and loosened his tie.

Ryan, the guy that had lost his wife, had stopped whimpering. He had stopped doing anything, in fact. He just sat in a corner of the cabin staring ahead of him, almost catatonic, probably playing over and over in his mind the moment that Gillian had been taken by something awful that came out of the wall. Ianto seriously hoped that they got him out of there soon, or perhaps the poor man would be caught in that hideous mind-loop for ever.

Simon and Andrew sat opposite Ianto, their arms looped together. It looked casual but he knew that they were each taking comfort from the contact. He thought about Jack, and hoped that he was all right.

He caught himself, and smiled. Like Jack wouldn't be all right.

'What's funny?'

It was Simon. It was a fair question. Anything that diverted them from craziness in here seemed fair.

How long had it been already?

'I know a joke about being stuck in a lift,' Ianto said. He didn't want to share Jack with them.

'Really?' said Andrew with zero interest. 'I know about you.'

'Me?'

'Torchwood. I've heard about you on that radio show. Abigail Crowe.'

Abigail Crowe ran a late-night internet radio show from somewhere in the city. She played a few records – weird stuff mostly – but generally it was talk. Phone-ins and guests – and, mostly, more weird stuff. It wasn't entirely unreasonable; after all, there was an awful lot of strange stuff that went down in and around Cardiff. Plenty of people noticed it now and again but, thankfully, not too many people put it all together or talked about it. Abigail Crowe tried to piece it all together, and she did so with the help of the people that rang her show.

A lot of them were nutters, of course – there were people who said they were witches and werewolves and some guy was on there a few weeks ago talking about how he had married a vampire.

Ianto listened to it occasionally, not that he was about to admit that to Andrew right now – and probably never to anyone in the team, either. And he had heard Abigail Crowe talk about Torchwood. People had heard the name; the police and the civil authorities were familiar with it – but no one actually knew exactly who they were or what they did. And that, of course, was always going to fuel talk. He had heard suggestions that they were some sort of black-ops outfit attached to the military, seeking out terrorist cells in Cardiff, and that was probably as close as anyone was ever going to get. For all Cardiff's weirdness over the last hundred years or so, no one was ever going to come out and say they were the city's answer to the Men in Black.

Even Abigail Crowe never said that. But she had hinted at it, once or twice.

'You're always around when something strange happens, aren't you?' said Andrew.

'I have no idea. That would depend on how often something strange actually happens,' Ianto pointed out.

Andrew shook his head and smiled. 'Come on. The Official Secrets Act doesn't apply in broken-down lifts. Everyone knows that.'

'I wouldn't know, I've never signed it.'

Andrew's eyebrows rose above his red glasses like French windscreen wipers. 'Really? So you're not part of the government? So what are you, then? Who do you work for?'

The absolute truth was that Ianto didn't really know. Torchwood had, of course, developed from the Torchwood Institute which was founded by Queen Victoria in 1879. He sometimes wondered if their pay cheques came from an office somewhere in Buckingham Palace. Maybe one day he, Jack and the others would all find themselves on the Honours List.

Most likely, posthumously.

Simon could tell that his partner was never going to get a

straight answer out of the Torchwood guy.

'OK,' he said. 'To be honest, I'm not interested in who you are, or what Torchwood is, but I think you do owe us some sort of explanation as to what's going on here. And just what happened to that poor man's wife.'

Ianto looked from Simon to Ryan, who, if he had heard a word of their conversation, made no sign of it.

'All right,' said Ianto. 'There's an alien in the building.'

He got no further than that because the elevator shook as if it had hit the side of a mountain – and the alien started to come through the roof.

TWENTY

The day that Ewan Lloyd met Besnik Lucca he had been moments from killing himself.

The trouble had started with the car crash. He had been at his office when the police showed up. He had been at his desk, immersed in figures relating to a major new construction project that one of the company's clients had under way in the Bay. There was something about the finances for the project that troubled him, had been nagging at him for days, but he was damned if he could put his finger on it. Being an accountant was no different from any other job, sometimes you developed a sixth sense. A doctor could look at a patient, a mechanic could listen to an engine, and sometimes an accountant could look at columns of figures that seemed to make sense and know that in some way they didn't. That was how he felt about the finances on the SkyPoint project. Something about them was wrong. He just couldn't see what it was.

But the police officer that came through his door wrecked

any interest he had in solving the puzzle.

Wendy and Alison had been taken to St Helen's Hospital. The driver of another car had hit them at a junction. Wendy had only cuts and bruises; Alison was in intensive care.

The next week had been a fog to him and he had been lost in it. He had found Wendy at the hospital and they had held each other and cried until they both thought their hearts would shatter. And they had sat beside their fragile, bruised, broken daughter in her ITU bed every day, listening to the machines and the computers that kept her alive and monitored her condition. They stayed there, and they waited for a sign of life, and they prayed.

Wendy had always believed in God. Her parents were Methodist, from somewhere out in the Valleys where Sunday mornings were still reserved for threats of Hell and Damnation. She had moved to work at the university in Cardiff and Ewan had met her in a sandwich shop one lunchtime. They started seeing each other, but it took him six months of bloody hard work to get her into bed, and afterwards she had cried because she had sinned. Ewan had held her then, and told her that he loved her and known that this time he meant it. They had married in a Cardiff church – Ewan always suspected that she felt too sullied by pre-marital sex to return to her home chapel – but Wendy never lost her commitment to God. Ewan never understood it – his family were nothing more than Christmas Christians. But for seven days, as he watched his little girl battle death, Wendy's faith kept him going.

But Alison came out of the coma. She survived. He didn't know if it was a miracle, medical science, or if his daughter simply had one kick-ass will to live. As she had lain in the coma, Wendy had told him that Alison had died at the scene of the crash for five minutes, but that the paramedics had brought her back. She had told him this to reassure him that their daughter was a fighter and that, if she had beaten death once, then she could survive the coma and would come back to them.

Ewan didn't care what had brought his daughter back from death – whether it had been God, science or voodoo – he just had his little girl back, and nothing else in the world mattered.

If this had been a show on TV, the tearful mum and dad that had watched over their still daughter for so long would have gone home with their miracle child as the credits rolled, and the audience would go put the kettle on with a warm glow in their stomach and maybe a little moisture in their eye. They would never stop to think about how things could turn to shit.

It started a couple of weeks later, when Wendy asked her daughter what she remembered about the crash. That wasn't what she really wanted to know, of course. Wendy had talked to Ewan late at night after Alison had gone to sleep, cuddled up to Mr Pickle in bed. Her daughter had died and now to Wendy – who had her daughter safe in bed upstairs and not in an undersized coffin beneath the ground – that was no longer something horrific, but a marvel. Alison had died and come back, and Wendy had read stories of the things that people had seen on the Other Side. It wasn't that her faith in the Afterlife needed confirmation, but her daughter had been in the presence of the Divine – who wouldn't want to know what that was like?

But Wendy hadn't liked what she heard.

That there was nothing beyond death but cold darkness.

Ewan understood the devastation of Wendy's world-view – more than that, her view of creation, of *everything* – and he tried to comfort her. He tried to tell her that maybe Alison was wrong. She was just a small child, after all. And she had gone through such a lot. Wendy couldn't expect her to really remember what happened to her being – her soul, whatever she wanted to call it – as the medics had worked on getting her heart to work again next to the car wreck. And at first he had thought that Wendy had understood that, and had accepted his logical reasoning. But then he had come to realise that that wasn't the case at all. He caught it in his wife's eyes sometimes when she didn't think he was looking, when she was watching Alison play with Mr Pickle.

Wendy hated their daughter.

More than that, she didn't believe that it was their daughter. What had come back in Alison's body was an agent of Satan, a demon that had come to destroy her faith by spreading lies about the end of hope.

The realisation that his wife was going mad and – more than that – that he couldn't cope, was what led Ewan Lloyd to the bottle and, ultimately, to the edge of what was to become Besnik Lucca's roof garden.

By that time Wendy was in hospital. It was a good place that had patience and cared. It was also costing Ewan a fortune that he couldn't afford. Things had got completely out of control – his drinking had put his business into a spiral that was accelerated by the cost of helping his wife, which made him drink more… He was a drunk drowning in a whirlpool. And, just then, the sooner it sucked him into oblivion, the better. Wendy was getting better, and Alison didn't seem to suspect anything of the truth about her mother's absence, but his family was shattered beyond repair all the same – because he hadn't been able to cope.

He knew they would all be better off without him. Wendy would land some good-looking bloke with a full head of hair and no beer belly – the kind of man she always should have been with – and Alison would get a stepfather who would be able to look after her properly. A real man who wouldn't just try to drink himself out of any problem that reared its head.

At around seventy metres off the ground, the wind whipped at you even on a calm day, and Ewan had been standing on the edge of the construction for quite a while, summoning up the last pulse of courage to take that final step. As he had edged towards the ledge, he had actually hoped that the force of the wind and the bottle and a half of scotch that had got him up there in the first place would combine to remove that final difficult step from his plan. Typical of the loser that he was, he thought, he even wanted the wind to do the tough part. He had kind of hoped that a good gust of wind would just unbalance him and a couple of seconds later he'd be on the pavement below, splattered like a lost ice cream. He supposed that it would be a strawberry or a raspberry ice cream. Something with a lot of red in it, anyway.

But the wind hadn't taken him to his death. Instead

Besnik Lucca had stood at his side and offered him a second chance.

Ewan had never laid eyes on Lucca until that moment, but of course he had heard the name; he knew that he was the major individual investor in the SkyPoint project and that it was his money that had been giving him a headache on the day that had set his life on course for the wastepipe. In between the time Alison had come out of her coma and the beginning of his realisation that his wife was going crazy, Ewan had started to ask questions about that money, and about Lucca. The fact that he hadn't found any satisfactory answers had, in its way, told him all he needed to know. The money was dirty; Lucca was a crook. Then his life had started to fall apart. And if the financial foundations of the SkyPoint job had also started to flake and crumble, everyone would have been buried in the rubble. So he had turned a blind eye to the financial irregularities, but he knew that Lucca had caught wind of his interest.

There had been a phone call.

It hadn't come to the office, and it hadn't been on his mobile. It had been at night, just after he had made sure Alison was OK in bed, as he did every night an hour or so after she had gone up. So it was around eight o'clock, and the phone in the hallway of his home started to ring.

None of his clients had his home number. If they needed to get him urgently outside of office hours then they had his mobile number, and he never turned that off. But Lucca had been sending him a message, and it wasn't contained in the words he spoke down the phone.

Lucca had identified himself and had said he wanted to

congratulate Ewan on the excellent work he was doing on the SkyPoint project. He was impressed by his diligence, he said. And also by his professional discretion. He hoped, he said, that Ewan would allow them both the opportunity to work together again in the future.

Ewan had understood every word that Lucca had not said.

I know where you live.

And when Lucca spoke into his ear as they stood together on the edge of oblivion above Cardiff Bay, Ewan recognised the accent immediately, and he felt the pressure of his hand on his shoulder.

He told Ewan that he could help him.

If he could not summon the courage to take his own life, Lucca would help him with the hand that he had placed on his shoulder.

Ewan looked down and saw that Lucca's gleaming black shoes were even closer than his own were to the edge and the fall into the old docklands below. He also saw that Lucca's other hand was extended towards him, as if he wanted Ewan to shake it.

Lucca told him that if he cared more for his family than he did for himself he would take the offered hand and he would work for him, and life would be good once again.

Ewan looked into Lucca's black eyes and shook his hand, and knew that he was more truly lost than ever.

And now, a year later, he sat on a whore's toilet seat with a broken ankle and his mobile phone in his hand, trying to reach the Devil.

Lucca picked up just as Ewan was about to give up,

ready to smash the phone against the bathroom's granite flooring.

'Hello, Ewan. Where are you?'

'What?' Ewan snarled. He was hurting and he was angry. Angrier with Lucca than he knew he had any sense to be. 'Don't tell me you can't bloody see me!'

Ewan knew all of Lucca's secrets. Not just the financial ones. He also knew about the cameras, even the one that watched his wife undress. When the Devil took your soul, he took everything else, too. And Lucca knew those secrets were safe with Ewan Lloyd. Weak men knew who their friends were and, if they forgot, their disposal was easy. A weak man who was also wise knew that, which was why he trusted Ewan Lloyd.

Lucca didn't respond to Ewan's anger, he said nothing and waited for the injured man to gather his wits.

'I'm on the eleventh floor,' he said in the end, trying to keep his voice low – the last thing he needed was that Torchwood guy catching him on the phone to Lucca. 'The whore's flat.' Ewan knew all about Marion Blake. He knew a lot of things about everyone that moved in to SkyPoint. Accountancy for Besnik Lucca covered a wide range of fields.

'Who is with you?' Lucca asked.

'Wendy and Alison. Marion. And the man with the Jap wife. Only I think that was some sort of cover.'

'Ewan, you are so perceptive,' Lucca taunted down the phone line.

'What the hell is going on, Besnik? Who are these people and what the hell is this talk about something being on the loose here? Ryan Freeman says something came through the wall and took his wife!'

'Everything is under control,' Lucca purred.

'Listen, Besnik, if there's anything dangerous up here, I want to get my wife and daughter out of here. You owe me that much.'

'*I owe you?*' Lucca said it slowly, disbelieving, without humour.

Ewan pushed a hand over his head, it came away wet with sweat and, for the first time in months, he needed a drink. 'I just want my little girl safe,' he said.

It went quiet on the other end of the line. For a long time Ewan thought he had pushed it too far. And Besnik Lucca wasn't the kind of man that you pushed at all.

Screw it, he thought. He didn't care, didn't care about anything except making sure Alison was safe. That was why he had refused to use the lifts. When the trouble had kicked off, he had known exactly what Lucca would do.

He knew all his secrets.

And Lucca knew him.

When he came back on the line, Lucca told Ewan exactly what he had to do if he wanted his help in getting Alison to safety.

And finally, though he had never meant to, Ewan threw up.

TWENTY-ONE

'Get behind me!' Ianto shouted. 'Get behind me, now!'

As he spoke, he pulled his automatic and wondered what the hell he was going to do with it. The thing that was coming through the roof of the elevator looked like slime, a glittering slime that undulated and glowed and spread across the ceiling.

It didn't look like bullets would do anything but slip through it. But he fired anyway.

The bang of the gun was deafening in the confinement of the elevator cabin. The sound waves slammed off the mirrored walls and hit him in the ears like hammer blows.

As he'd expected, the four bullets he fired punched holes in the ceiling, but did nothing to the creature that clung to it.

It did encourage Andrew and Simon to do what he'd told them, however, and they crowded behind him in a corner of the elevator – not that it was going to do any of them any good, and they all knew it.

Ryan had stayed where he was, crumpled on the floor, the slightest inclination of his head was the only suggestion that he was aware that anything at all had changed – never mind the cabin being invaded by some oozing alien.

'Jesus Christ! What is it?' Andrew gasped behind Ianto.

'What does it matter?' came pragmatic Simon. 'We're dead.'

Ianto stared at the thing that clung to the ceiling. It had no eyes, but he couldn't shake the feeling that they were watching each other. His mind raced, trying to think of something he could do. He knew there was nothing. Instead, he tried to think of something that would make the last moments more bearable. He thought of Jack.

The creature began to slide down the far corner of the cabin, collecting there.

Ianto wondered how death would feel, if it was as bad as Owen said it was. It hadn't only been Owen, of course. Before him they had brought people back with the first resurrection glove. Only ever for two minutes. But they never said anything about angels and harps or pearly gates. And as Ianto had watched their time run out on his pocket watch, they had never wanted to go back there.

He watched the creature slide down the wall of the elevator and thought that there wouldn't be much left of him to resurrect, even if they still had one of the gloves.

He kind of wished he'd had time for one more cup of coffee.

Then Ryan pulled his shivering body off the floor and threw himself at the creature, screaming his wife's name.

There wasn't time to pull him back. And what would

have been the point?

Ryan seemed to sink into the creature and as Ianto watched they could see him screaming, but heard nothing – he got the impression that he wasn't even there with them any more, but that what they were seeing was some sort of image being transmitted from another place. And then the whole thing drew back out through the wall leaving no trace of itself, or the man that it had taken.

For a moment, Ianto and the other two men didn't move. When they found that they could, they still couldn't speak.

Ianto had seen strange, strange things. But somehow this was stranger than any. His mind felt momentarily overloaded.

It was Simon that spoke first. 'Am I going mad?'

Andrew wrapped his arms around him and kissed him hard. 'I don't care. As long as I'm alive, I don't care.'

Simon touched Ianto's sleeve. 'Do you think he did that for us? Ryan. Did he save us?'

Ianto didn't know if Ryan had been a hero, or had just thrown himself after his wife, but he nodded.

'He saved us,' he said. 'For now.'

He looked at the ceiling and let that sink in with his two companions. It didn't take long.

'It's going to come back, isn't it?' said Andrew.

Ianto was matter-of-fact. 'Probably. It knows we're here.'

'Canned meat,' Simon observed.

It made Ianto smile. 'That's right. We have to get out. Now, one of you give me a leg up.'

There was a hatch in the roof. From his jacket, Ianto took a small torch and, stowing the automatic in his belt, he slid his foot into the stirrup of Simon's interlocked hands and boosted himself through the inspection cover, and into the elevator shaft.

He got himself up onto the elevator roof and turned on the torch. He'd never been on top of an elevator before and wasn't sure of what he'd find. He wasn't sure if he might find the wall-walker up there chowing down on Ryan Freeman. All he did find was an unimpressive and dirty lift shaft.

He had hoped there might have been some sort of ladder on the wall. He had presumed that someone had to make inspections sometimes, but maybe they just rode the roof of the lift, or they abseiled down from the top of the shaft. Or maybe they just didn't bother. Anyway, there was no ladder.

'What can you see?' Simon called from below.

'Nothing encouraging,' Ianto told him.

That wasn't entirely true: he could see a set of doors that would lead onto the next floor up. The problem was going to be how they got to them. He was pretty sure that he'd be able to prise them open, but the prospect of standing on thin air while he did that was the disheartening part.

Ianto looked at his watch and wondered how long it would take the creature to digest Ryan, and then come back for more.

And then he saw something to really worry him. The elevator was suspended on a cable. It was thick and would take a lot of weight and a lot of wear. But it looked like when Ianto had fired through the roof of the cabin a couple of his bullets had shorn through the cable.

He could see it shredding slowly.

If he needed confirmation, a dozen metal strands suddenly gave way and the elevator car lurched.

He heard the men inside scream, and Ianto held on for grim life.

'What the hell was that?' he heard a terrified Simon yell.

The car had fallen half a metre at most, but that only meant that there was another thirty or more metres yet for it to fall. And the cable was stretching and straining.

The good news was that the fall had dropped the elevator alongside a set of doors that Ianto could reach from the roof. But the guys inside were going to have to climb up here to use them – and that meant a lot of clambering about. He wasn't sure if the damaged, straining cable was going to be able to take it. But the only alternative was a long drop.

Ianto looked at the slowly shearing cable and moved carefully, stretching down into the cabin to reach for Andrew's hand while he told the two men what they were up against.

'Sod it,' said Simon. 'Sometimes you just wish you'd stayed in bed.'

Ianto hauled Andrew up first, and listened to the sound of the stretching metal fibres in the elevator cable as Andrew helped Simon. If the whole thing went, Ianto thought, it was going to be a toss-up which happened first – the car dropped and smashed them to bits eight or nine floors below; or the flying metal cable decapitated them.

At least he had more of a choice of deaths than five minutes earlier.

Ianto told Simon and Andrew to stay where they were. The less movement there was, the more time they might have. He crawled toward the partially exposed doors and tried to push them apart.

They weren't having it.

Beneath him, he felt the elevator car groan, its weight pulling against the fraying metal threads of the cable.

'Hurry up!' he heard Andrew urging, his voice trembling.

Ianto felt sorry for them. The closest these two had probably ever come to death was crossing the road at rush hour. Now, inside five minutes, they'd been nearly chewed up by something that came through the wall and the odds were they were going to end up smashed to pieces at the bottom of an elevator shaft.

Get a move on!

Ianto got his fingertips on the steel door edges and pulled, but being half-crouched on top of a lift car was far from the optimum position to really get his back into the job. He heard movement behind him and felt the elevator shift a little more. Simon and Andrew were alongside him now and without a word, all three men started to pull on the door.

Ianto felt it start to give, and his fingers got a better purchase. Over his head, he heard the sound of another wire snapping in the cable.

'Put your backs into it, boys!' he growled, and strained against the doors.

Beneath him he could feel the elevator car trembling against the weakening hold of the failing cable. They only had a few seconds…

Push!

And the doors slid apart, just a little – just enough.

'Quickly, now,' Ianto ordered, and Simon pushed Andrew through the doors. There was the sound of him tumbling to the floor in the darkness on the other side, then Simon went through.

And that was when the cable snapped with the sound of a gunshot, and the elevator car fell from beneath Ianto's feet. Instinctively, he threw out his hands and caught the edge of one of the doors.

A moment later, he heard the elevator hit the bottom of the shaft with the sound of an express train hitting a mountain side. There was no explosion, but he felt a wave of oily air and dust brush past him. Then Simon and Andrew were hauling him between the doors and onto the thick pile carpet of the sixth floor.

Ianto rolled over and the carpet felt as soft as meadow grass and the still air of the ghost-lit corridor as good as the fresh breeze of a summer's day.

TWENTY-TWO

Owen had made two charges. The ingredients were tightly packed into a couple of small pickle jars that he'd found in Marion Blake's fridge. He'd punctured their lids with a corkscrew and used some twine he'd found in another drawer as a couple of fuses. He wasn't sure what she ordinarily used the twine for but figured that of all the SkyPoint residents that could have ignored the fire alarm, he was glad that it had been an S&M call girl. As he set the makeshift explosives aside on Marion's kitchen work surface, he caught the face of his watch, and couldn't quite believe that a part of him was actually wondering if he was still going to have time to go looking for the man-munching twins from Constantine's coffee shop.

Hey, what else was a guy who didn't sleep going to do once he'd got the Lloyds and Mistress Marion to safety, then made it up to the penthouse and kicked Lucca's arse into a twenty-five storey freefall?

It had taken him half an hour to mix the chemicals. You had to be careful around explosives, especially the homemade variety. There was a reason so many terrorists had only one eye or used hooks for hands. Owen hadn't wanted to blow his face off. A talking corpse was one thing – you could get away with that – but a talking skull? That was going to make people take a second look in any light.

'Are you finished?'

It was Marion. She had used the time to shed her work clothes. She hadn't quite gone back to the Mary Whitehouse look, but they wouldn't have thrown her out of church, either. She was curled up on the sofa at what she clearly hoped was a safe distance.

Owen noticed that they were alone. 'What happened to Alison and her mum?'

Marion cocked her thumb towards her bedroom. 'I think Wendy took Alison to lie down. It looked like you were going to be a while.'

Just as likely, they were under the bed in there in case the madman with the busted hand blew them all to hell, he thought.

'What about Ewan?'

'He hasn't come out of the loo yet.'

Owen didn't feel his blood chill, but he felt distinctly uncomfortable. 'Are you sure?'

'Of course I'm sure. I'm telling you, if he's made a mess in there…'

He had heard Wendy tell her about what was supposed to be stalking SkyPoint. If the significance of something coming through walls at people and Ewan not having shown after half an hour in the bathroom hadn't clicked with Marion, Owen wondered if he should be checking her over for signs of something nasty as a result of her profession.

He got up and walked towards the bathroom, dreading what he might find there. He rapped on the door, and called out Ewan's name.

'Yeah – yeah, I'm coming!'

Owen felt the tension fall off him like a heavy coat. 'OK, well hurry up. We need to get moving. And I need to splint up that ankle first.'

The bathroom door opened and Ewan stood in the doorway, his injured ankle held slightly off the ground. His shirt was damp down the front. Owen guessed that he must have been sick after all. He certainly didn't look any better, his face was pale and shone with sweat, and his eyes were red-rimmed, like he'd been crying, and wouldn't stop moving. This was a guy that was very close to the edge.

'Here, let me give you a hand,' said Owen, and he put one arm across his shoulders and helped Ewan as best he could back through to the lounge.

As they went, Owen spoke to him gently. It was the kind of voice he had used a lifetime ago sitting next to nervous patients in ward beds. 'Take it easy, Ewan. Everything's going to be all right, I promise. I'm going to get you and your family out of here. Believe me, we do this sort of thing all the time.'

They reached the couch, and Owen let him down gently. Ewan didn't look all that comforted.

Owen glanced up at Marion. 'Have you got any painkillers around? Paracetamol? Hash? I think he could use something.'

'I think I can find something,' she said hesitantly and left the lounge to go get it.

Owen gave Ewan a playful wink. 'Let's hope she finds the good stuff.'

Then he picked up the two whips, moved back across to the kitchen and selected a knife from the rack she had fitted there. He could have performed surgery with them. All he needed to do was separate the whips from their handles. The knife he chose did the job easily. He took the handles and the whips back to Ewan and started to bind the handles into place with the first of the whips.

'This is going to hurt a bit,' he warned.

Ewan said nothing.

The next thing Owen knew was that Ewan had the other whip around his throat and was pulling it tight. Very tight.

The immediate thought that shot through Owen's mind was that generally since he had been reanimated as a walking, talking corpse the advantages of his condition were comprehensively outnumbered on a day-to-day basis by the ball-crushing downsides. Right now, though, a real bonus was the fact that he no longer needed to breathe – which meant that any attempt to strangle him was going to be pretty futile.

Briefly, he thought about just waiting it out – it wouldn't take too long before Ewan got bored or, in his condition, exhausted. Then Owen thought about his neck and how – whether Ewan meant it or not – snapping it would be all too easy. And if Owen had to be a living corpse, he'd rather be part of the walking-dead rather a quadriplegic cadaver for the rest of his unnatural life.

So he fought back hard, and broke Ewan's nose with his head.

Noses are pretty easy to break, and there wasn't much in Ewan's that was going to do Owen any harm. A broken nose also hurt like hell and, as Owen expected, Ewan gave up on throttling him pretty fast.

Owen just wished he'd had a gun to push into Ewan's bloody face when he turned on him and demanded to know what the hell was going on.

The blood from Ewan's smashed nose was mixed with tears as he shuddered with grief and shame, and tried to protect himself with hands that shook like fragile leaves.

'I'm sorry! I'm sorry!' he wailed.

Owen grabbed the other man's shirt front, and would have made a fist to threaten him with – only he remembered that hand was busted and bandaged.

'You're sorry?'

'He told me he would get Wendy and Alison out if I killed you!'

'Who?'

'Lucca! Besnik Lucca! I work for him, God help me! I'm an accountant, not a killer! I couldn't – I couldn't have done it! But he said—'

'You've spoken to him? When?'

Ewan pulled the mobile phone from his trouser pocket. 'In the bathroom.'

Owen grabbed the phone and saw Lucca's number. His mind raced. There had to be a way he could use this.

Then Wendy burst into the lounge and screamed.

Alison had gone.

TWENTY-THREE

The darkest time in Toshiko Sato's life had been the months she had spent in the UNIT cell. There had been no real bed, the toilet had been little more than a hole in the ground, and the food had been some tasteless gruel that had been nutritionally designed to do no more than keep her alive. But the worst part was that she had no hope. No one knew she was there and no one there was interested in her account of why she had stolen the plans for the sonic modulator. She had believed that she would die there.

But Jack had rescued her then and, as she sat bound to the chair in Besnik Lucca's sumptuous penthouse, she knew that he and the others would do everything they could to do so again. The difference was that back then Jack had been in control. He had had the influence to walk into that UNIT incarceration facility and spring her to work for him. At SkyPoint, Lucca was the man in charge. That meant Jack might need some help.

Lucca's men had secured her to the chair with plastic

cable-ties. They were the same things that the military used to detain prisoners. Thin strips of tough plastic that were less bulky to carry than handcuffs, and did the job better. Once they were tightened up, the only way they could be released was with a knife, and if you struggled against them they cut into your flesh. Lucca's men were used to this sort of thing – they had secured each of her arms to the chair at her wrist and with another cable-tie over her forearm. Her ankles had also been cable-tied to the chair legs. Like this, she wasn't going anywhere; wasn't going to be any help to the others at all.

The one thing that they couldn't tie up, however, was her mind. And that was all she needed to try and get free.

Lucca and his goons seemed to have lost all interest in her lately – which had been a relief. Lucca had become absorbed in watching the progress of his game on the floors below him. He had brought the images up on the huge television set in the lounge and now lay sprawled on the couch with a remote control flicking between the hidden cameras. But for the glass of champagne in his other hand and the opulent surroundings, he would have looked like just about any other late-night channel grazer looking for something on TV to get them through their insomnia.

He had howled with delight when he saw Gwen demolish the door to the stairs with a hail of bullets, and he had hissed with pantomime fury when Ianto had survived the crashing elevator. But he was completely relaxed, Toshiko noted, utterly confident of his invulnerability – both from the Torchwood team and whatever was also out there stalking the building's occupants.

Besnik Lucca was, without doubt, a psychopath. He was a man without conscience, whose only drive was personal gratification without any care for the cost to others. A man whose narcissism was such that he believed he was better than anyone, more beautiful, more powerful and – quite definitely – unassailable by anything, even a creature that could walk through walls and reduce you to a pile of cellular crap.

To put it another way, he was mad.

Maybe that could work for her.

The two henchmen had disappeared from the apartment – maybe they were out in the roof garden, smoking. As long as they weren't in Lucca's small control room.

That was where he had gone when he turned the power off to the rest of the building. That was where she was going to have to get to, to turn it back on.

They would come after her, of course. But as long as they didn't get to her for just a couple of minutes... that was all it would take for Jack to realise that the power was back on and to take an elevator to the penthouse floor. Lucca wouldn't open the doors – as he hadn't for her until she surrendered her gun – but that wouldn't be a problem for Jack. He had a gadget that would pop the lock on the elevator as easily as cracking a bottle of beer.

A couple of minutes, maybe less.

Toshiko started to rock the chair. It was big and heavy, an industrial steel frame with a leather seat and back. Stylish, but also somehow a bit like something from a torture chamber. She was only small – it took her a while to work up the momentum to get the chair moving.

Lucca looked away from the TV as she crashed heavily to the floor. He stood up, frowning, and moved slowly towards her. Toshiko watched him come closer, one side of her body hurting with the impact.

Lucca started to shake his head, pitifully. 'Whatever are you trying to do, Toshiko?'

Toshiko grunted something behind the gag in her mouth, and struggled against the cable-ties. It was just for effect, but it hurt like hell, all the same.

Lucca took the chair and set it straight. He did it easily. He was a strong man.

Toshiko looked into his eyes and said something else behind the gag. Lucca slipped his hands behind her head and released the gag.

'Now,' he said patiently, as if talking to a child, 'what is it you want to say?'

'Save my friends, please.'

Lucca's mouth curled. 'What?'

'I know what's out there. The thing that comes through the walls. And they can't stop it with bullets.'

'Oh, I know.' Lucca smiled. He had seen what happened when the tall one dressed like a tailor's dummy had fired at the creature in the elevator.

'It will kill them.'

'That's the general idea,' he said.

'But you could save them,' she said, anxiously. 'We could save them. I can save you.'

That intrigued him. 'What do you mean?'

'I'm a scientist. I know what that creature is, *and* I know how we could make your penthouse invulnerable to it.'

'It is invulnerable. If it hadn't been it would have come for me before now.'

'Why would it? There were plenty of people on the lower floors before. But most of them have gone. Yes, it might pick off those that are left and my friends first, but then it's going to come here, Lucca. And you won't be able to keep it out without me.'

He looked at her suspiciously. 'What makes you so clever?'

Toshiko pursed her lips, impatient. 'Do I have to go through my CV? Would you even understand it?' she asked.

Lucca regarded her for a full ten seconds without a word then drew something from his pocket. Without taking his eyes off her, he brushed it with his thumb and a long steel blade sprang into his hand. Toshiko couldn't help but look at the switchblade. The steel was dark and old and its edge was nicked and worn. It looked like it might have come with Lucca when he first escaped his homeland, and she didn't want to think what it had probably been used for. Lucca watched her and read every thought that went through her mind. He had seen the same reaction – and worse – a thousand times.

'You are very beautiful, Toshiko,' he said gently. 'You shouldn't try my patience.'

'I'm sorry,' she said. 'But I don't want to die, either. That's why I want to help you.'

Lucca crouched before her, and ran the knife's edge gently over her arm. She felt the blade pass lightly over her bare skin, the sensation was electric, like a kiss.

'Suppose I said you could save yourself – and me – but not your friends?'

Her eyes had been following the knife as it caressed her arm; now it paused at the cable-tie over her forearm. She looked at him.

'I want to live,' she said.

Lucca looked at her, then kissed her on the lips. It was gentle. Like a lover's parting. Then he folded the knife away.

'I'm sorry to disappoint you, Toshiko,' he said. 'But you're not going to.'

TWENTY-FOUR

They were on the twentieth floor when Gwen saw the shadow of the Weevil.

'What was that?'

She and Jack had been taking the concrete steps two at a time, lighting their way with their flashlights, and their guns held aloft. They didn't know what they might run into on those shadowy stairs, but Gwen hadn't expected to catch sight of a Weevil.

'Where?' Jack asked, spinning around in the stairwell, sweeping the dull concrete walls with light. All he saw was the number 20 on the door to the floor and more stairs.

'Out there,' she said, and edged towards the door, and looked out through its porthole window. Beyond the glass the floor was lit eerily green by the emergency lights, and nothing seemed to be moving. 'I thought I saw a Weevil.'

Jack looked from Gwen to the stillness beyond. He saw nothing.

'It was just a shadow,' she said, starting to doubt herself

now. 'Maybe I imagined it.'

Then Jack saw something move out there. Again, just a shadow. But there was something. Maybe someone hadn't got out when the alarm went off; maybe they had been trapped when Lucca locked off the doors.

Maybe they should take a look.

The locking mechanism to the doors was on their side, so it only took one bullet instead of a full double clip to get through.

The sound of the shot bounced off the concrete walls of the stairwell and seemed to echo all the way up to the top of the shaft. Their ears were still ringing as they stepped into the carpeted corridor.

'Hello?' Jack called. 'Hello? Anybody here?'

The silence was as deafening as the gunshot had been.

Jack started to move slowly along the corridor, the Webley held before him in both hands. Gwen followed, her eyes searching the gloomy green-cast shadows for movement. Her insides felt like they had bunched themselves up into a defensive ball, every nerve in her body felt like piano wire. She didn't like it. She'd been in situations like this a hundred times and more, but she had never felt like this before. The gun grip felt slick in her hands and she realised that her palms were sweating.

As they turned a corner in the corridor, Jack caught her eye. There was more light here, there was a big window that looked out over the Bay below. Most of the restaurants and bars were turning off their lights now – Jack guessed it was something like three in the morning – but there was still enough light to tell that Gwen was scared.

'Are you OK?' he asked.

'No,' she said.

'If it's any comfort, me neither.'

He could feel sweat trickling down his back. It was a sensation he hadn't felt in a long time. A gut-gnawing fear that started in your belly and spread out through your nervous system like a virus. The kind of fear that, if you didn't get a hold on it, could paralyse you. That wasn't the good kind of fear that pumped you with adrenalin and supercharged you to fight or run. It was the kind that got you killed.

Jack didn't understand it. Weevil hunts were almost a downtime diversion for Torchwood. The Cardiff sewers had been crawling with them for so long now that they were soon going to be more a job for the city's sanitation department than them. If anything ever got routine for Jack's team, it was hunting out Weevils. You didn't get blasé about one and a half metres of muscle and teeth that just lived for tearing your throat out, but you got accustomed to them the same way an alligator wrangler could work around ninety kilos of snapping jaw and not get chewed. You developed a life-preserving respect for them, but you weren't scared of them like this.

'There!' Gwen cried, and opened fire.

Jack spun around with the Webley cocked, but saw nothing.

Gwen had fired four rounds. She stopped, breathing in the cordite of spent shells. Ahead of them she had shattered one of the apartment doors, but there was no sign of a Weevil.

Jack ran on down the corridor. Maybe she had winged it.

Gwen heard something move in the apartment and kicked open the door, holding her gun level with her face. She could feel the heat of the automatic's barrel gently warming her skin. She realised that she was cold. Cold, yet sweating – that was not good.

The apartment was dimly illuminated by what was left of the lights in the Bay. It occurred to her that there might be someone in there taking refuge. She swept the apartment with her flashlight, and called out but got no answer.

Cautiously, she moved through the apartment and checked the bedroom and the bathroom. There was no one there, not even a cat. But she'd have sworn on her mother's life that she had heard something in there.

She was sure she had seen a Weevil in the shadows outside the door when she opened fire. If she had just winged it and it got away in the gloom it was bloody lucky – she never missed.

She rubbed at her eyes. Her vision was blurring a little. She was tired and stressed out.

Christ, she could do with a drink.

She played the flashlight across the apartment again and saw a collection of bottles standing on a small table. One vodka would steady her nerves.

Just a small one.

She put her gun down on the table and picked up the bottle and poured out a large measure. She picked the glass up.

And that was when the Weevil came through the apartment door.

Gwen caught it out of the corner of her eye and cursed herself for dropping her guard.

Jesus, she was tired.

It was tall for a Weevil, but was dressed in the same boiler suit they all seemed to wear. It had no ears to speak of, just holes low down at the sides of its head and its eyes were buried in hollows punched in either side of the snub nose. It was an ugly brute – all of them were – and it snarled at her with a mouth full of savage teeth.

It leaped towards her.

Gwen threw aside the vodka glass and lunged for her gun.

It was the vodka that saved Jack.

If Gwen hadn't put the Glock down, she would have shot the Weevil through the head, and that would have put Jack on the floor and ruined the apartment's expensive white carpet with his brains. His brains would have grown back together pretty quickly, of course, the shattered skull would have rebuilt itself and he would have been good as new in a few minutes, but a bullet through the brain always scrambled him up a bit for a while and right now he needed to be thinking straight.

Because something was messing with their heads.

Jack threw himself to the floor before Gwen could fire and screamed out, 'Gwen, it's me! It's Jack!'

The Weevil had disappeared, but Gwen held the gun steady, ready for it to come at her again.

'Jack, there's a Weevil!'

He was crouched behind the couch now. He knew it would be no defence against the automatic clip she was likely to fire if she got it into her head that the Weevil was also down there, but he figured it was just safer if she didn't see him right now.

'No, Gwen. There is no Weevil!'

'What are you talking about?' she snapped, and swung from side to side, just in case the Weevil was trying to work its way around her.

'Remember Lucca said he had this place well fortified. I think he's got some sort of psychotropic gas on this floor. When he initiated his defences, the gas would have been released. It's winding us up, making us see things.'

'No, Jack. You're talking crap.'

'Listen to yourself, Gwen. It's affecting your reason. Ask yourself, why the hell would there be Weevils on the twentieth floor of this place? How would they even get in here? It's built like Fort Knox.'

'I saw a Weevil, Jack! What the hell's got into you? What have they done to you?'

Jack could feel any hold on Gwen slipping away from him. If he was right – and he knew that he was – he hadn't felt as scared as this since that last god-awful day on the Boeshane Peninsular. Whatever Lucca had in the air here was eating into their minds, and it was not only making Gwen hallucinate, but also turning her paranoid.

'Who are *they*, Gwen?'

'You know. Don't pretend, Jack!'

'Gwen, listen to me, please. Concentrate on what I say, Lucca has released some sort of hallucinogen into the air. It's part of his defences. To turn us on each other. You've got to fight it, Gwen, and we have to get off this floor. Now!'

Jack stayed behind the couch and waited for his words to get through to her. He counted the seconds, and fought the fear and dread that still surged through his own body.

When he had run after the phantom Weevil he had seen that there was nowhere for it to go, and had forced himself to be logical. He wasn't always the most logical man – sometimes defying logic could save your life; could save a planet – but sometimes logic was a piece of lifesaving driftwood when reality was getting wrecked around you.

Like now.

There had been nowhere for the Weevil to run and he knew that Weevils didn't walk through walls. And when he'd forced his own haunted anxiety aside he realised there was no way that there had been any Weevil there when Gwen had fired. Apart from anything else, Gwen didn't miss.

And, when you got down to it, Jack Harkness does not get frightened by shadows.

But Gwen hadn't answered him yet, hadn't realised that he was her friend, the man she trusted with her life beyond anyone else in the world – maybe even more than her husband.

'Gwen?' he said, his worries building to new levels.

She answered him with a burst of fire from the automatic on machine setting that shredded the couch to splintered wood and torn foam.

But Jack had moved by then. He'd heard the click as Gwen had put the gun into machine pistol mode and had dived across the apartment and rolled to his feet as she ejected the spent magazine from the gun and reached for a new one.

She was wild-eyed and trembling with psychotic adrenalin.

And Jack knew this was his only chance.

He aimed the Webley and fired six times.

Gwen ducked as the apartment's window shattered behind her, and Jack lunged for her, kicked the automatic out of her hand and put his arm around her waist, dragging her to the devastated window as the wind caught their hair.

She struggled, but Jack got his arms around Gwen, pinning her hands against her body as he threw them both against the wall next to the window.

'Breathe, Gwen,' he said. 'Breathe it in. Deep breaths.'

And as he filled his own lungs with the cool fresh air that blew in over the Bay he could already feel the tension in his body starting to ease.

He could feel her holding her breath, refusing to give in to him, still somehow believing that he was an enemy, but he held her tight, pinned her to the wall and knew that any moment she was going to start to breathe, and then they were going to get through it.

'Hey,' he whispered in her ear. 'I said big breaths. I want big breaths. I really love big breaths.'

And the pure air must have already started working on her, because she laughed. And then she was breathing deeply, filling her lungs with the air that smelled salty and of the sea, and of freedom.

'I'm OK,' she said at last.

Jack continued to hold her tight.

'I said I'm all right, Jack.'

'I know,' he said. 'But you know me – any excuse.'

'I'm a married woman now, Captain Harkness,' she said playfully, and escaped his arms.

He looked at her as the wind did things with her hair, and she looked beautiful. In all his years and travels, there hadn't been many women that compared to Gwen Cooper.

She saw him looking and felt uncomfortable in his gaze. He saw it, and stooped down to get her gun. He handed it back to her.

'We should go,' he said, quickly. 'Just try not to breathe too deeply till we hit the next floor.'

'Jack,' she said.

He was already halfway across the apartment. He turned back. 'What?'

She hesitated, and he could see that something was on her mind, maybe something about the way she had seen him look at her. Then she gave him a hard look. 'That kick really hurt, you know.'

TWENTY-FIVE

'Alison's gone! She's gone!'

Wendy was crying and screaming as she rushed out of the bedroom. Owen still stood over her bloody, shaking husband. Marion appeared from the bathroom with painkillers in one hand and a spliff in the other. Owen no longer felt like easing Ewan's pain, especially since he had just increased it by the increment of a broken nose.

'What's happened? What's going on?' Marion demanded.

'It's taken Alison,' Wendy screamed.

Owen looked from her to Ewan and saw the fat man that had just tried to kill him come apart at the seams. For an instant he wished he hadn't broken the bastard's nose – he had only been trying to save his little girl. And now she had been taken from him.

'Wendy,' Ewan croaked, his voice distorted by his smashed nose.

She went to him and they held each other and shook

with shared grief. Owen doubted that she had even noticed the blood.

Owen grabbed an ornament from a shelf – he didn't see what it was, he didn't care – and threw it against the wall with all the force he could find. It detonated. Whatever it had been was shattered beyond recognition. His foot lashed out and kicked over Marion Blake's coffee table. He looked for something else to destroy and saw Marion's pale frightened face.

He shook his head, suddenly impotent and weak. 'I'm sorry.'

He fell heavily into a chair. 'I'm sorry,' he said again.

Owen had told them he would get them to safety. He had promised himself that Alison wouldn't go back into the darkness – not for years, if he could help it. Not until the darkness took her as naturally as it took anyone.

He looked at Wendy and Ewan. Their hearts were breaking. Not just because they had lost their little girl but because they knew to where she had gone. This time for good.

Thank God at least they didn't know how her remains would look when Torchwood found them. If Torchwood survived.

'What happened?' he asked eventually.

It took a while before Wendy could find her voice through the sobs. 'I took her to lie down. It looked like you were going to be a while, and I didn't want her around while you were making explosives. We lay down on the bed together and – oh, God forgive me – I fell asleep. Only a few minutes – it could only have been a few minutes. But she'd gone!'

Owen got up and walked into the bedroom where they'd been sleeping. The bed was made, but he could see the impressions left by two bodies that had recently lain there. One was smaller than the other.

He stood in the doorway and ran his eyes over the room. Nothing had been disturbed. There were no signs of the thing that had come through the wall. But then, there never was any sign.

Alison Lloyd had been taken without trace.

And that made him think.

Mr Pickle, the pixie doll, had gone, too. He remembered that she'd had it when he'd seen her on the thirteenth floor. He remembered she was hanging on to it the same way that Wendy hung on to her, like she would never let her go.

If the wall-walker had taken Alison while she was sleeping, why would it also take a rag doll? Whatever the wall-walker was, it was clear that it needed human cellular matter – presumably as some sort of food. Non-human matter, like the estate agent's clown cufflinks got left as waste. He supposed that Alison might have been hanging on to the doll in her sleep, but then why hadn't the thing taken Wendy, as well?

He looked around the room again, then got down on his hands and knees and saw what he was looking for. Under the bed, the cover to the air duct had been removed. The duct was small, but not too small for a six-year-old child and her rag doll pixie.

Owen felt a thrill of excitement burst through his body and he shoved the bed away from the wall and pushed his head into the duct. He couldn't see a thing in there – it was pitch black. Fleetingly he wondered what the hell Alison found so fascinating in a claustrophobic black hole like this after where she had been. But her mother had already told him that she used SkyPoint's ducting like her own private travelator.

He called into the ducting: 'Alison! Alison, are you there!'

His own voice came back at him. But nothing else.

He heard someone behind him and turned to see Wendy in the doorway. Her face was tear-stained, but he recognised renewed hope there, as well.

'I think she and Mr Pickle just went for a look around the pixie tunnels again,' he said, getting to his feet.

As he did so, Wendy lunged towards the ventilator and called her daughter's name as he had. There was still no reply. She tried again, this time screaming, angry and desperate; 'Alison! Alison, come back here, now!'

Owen took her by the shoulders and eased her away from the duct. 'It's OK, Wendy. We can find her. She's still alive, that's the main thing.'

She was crying again. He felt her body shaking against his and he put his arms around her.

'Where do you think she'll go? Back to your apartment? Her bedroom, maybe?'

Wendy shook her head, trying to calm herself down and think straight for the sake of her little girl.

'Maybe. Maybe,' she said. 'I don't know. Or there's the SkyPark.'

The indoor garden area where she had been reading the story of Rapunzel to Mr Pickle.

'OK,' Owen said. 'Stay here with Ewan and Marion. I'm going to go and find her. Don't worry, she'll be safe with me.'

But as he got up, Wendy caught his hand. 'No,' she said. 'I have to come with you.'

Owen thought about telling her that she couldn't; that there was something out there that came at you through walls and turned you into jelly shit. But she knew most of that already, and she was going to be no safer in the flat with Marion and Ewan than she was looking for her daughter.

'OK, then,' he said. 'But do exactly as I say. And when I say it.'

She nodded and Owen took her into the lounge and let her tell Ewan and Marion what had happened, while he found a bag that he could sling over his shoulder. Into it he put the two charges, a gas kitchen lighter, and one of Marion's big knives wrapped in a tea towel to save stabbing himself. He then slipped Ewan's mobile into the back pocket of his jeans. Maybe a direct line to the madman on the top floor would come in useful. He also found a torch.

'Come on,' he told Wendy. 'We ought to get going.'

She nodded and joined him at the door.

'Owen.'

He saw that it was Ewan. His broken nose had stopped bleeding, but he hadn't wiped away any of the mess.

'Please find my daughter,' he said.

'Take the painkillers,' Owen told him. 'We'll be back as soon as we can.'

And he led Wendy out of the apartment and towards the stairs. He tried the door first, in case it wasn't locked. But it was. He took out the first of his charges, set it by the door and told Wendy to take cover further down the corridor before he lit the twine fuse with the kitchen lighter. The twine burned with a fast yellow flame and Owen ran.

He knew the chemistry of bomb building, but he had never had to employ it before – Torchwood tended to be a more professional and high-tech in its approach to blowing things up. Nor were a teaspoon and a set of kitchen scales any sensible replacement for the precision of lab equipment. He knew the bomb would work, he just wasn't sure if it would take out the door – or the wall with it.

The explosion caught Owen halfway along the passageway and threw him off his feet. He rolled towards the wall at the far end. He managed to stop himself and lay there for a moment, not daring to raise his head in case his body lifted up without it.

Wendy had taken cover in a doorway, and the percussion of the blast had thrown him clear past her. He heard her crawling towards him through the dust and murk of the emergency lights.

'Are you all right?' she demanded, her eyes wide with fright.

'Do I look all right?' he asked her without moving, pleased that at least his vocal cords were working, which suggested his head was still attached to his neck. Beyond that, it was anybody's guess.

'Well, you're still alive,' she said, trying for a smile.

'Yeah,' said Owen, and sat up straight. He brought his hands up in front of him – one was still mangled, the other looked OK. At least they both remained attached. And he found that he could still stand. And his head was facing the right way.

'Well, seeing as we're still in business, let's take a look, shall we?'

He picked up his bag of goodies and walked towards the stairway. The door was a smoking, shattered skeleton. The steps ran into darkness beyond them. Owen turned on the torch and led Wendy after him.

It didn't take them long to reach the thirteenth floor, and Owen saw that Jack and Gwen had found their own way of getting through a locked door. It made him ache for his own gun. He doubted that 10mm shells would be much protection against the thing that he had seen come through the wall, but there was also a psychopath living on the top floor who probably had a bunch of knuckle-draggers doing his work for him. Owen had an uncomfortable feeling that they could be hanging around SkyPoint, too. If Lucca was treating Torchwood's interest as a test of his defences then why wouldn't he also despatch some tooled-up muscle into the arena? That was why he had taken Marion's carving knife with him, but his modified Glock was going to be a lot handier in a fire-fight.

They reached the Lloyds' apartment, and Wendy opened the door. Everything was dark in there as she slipped in and called out for her daughter.

There was no answer. Owen knew that if she wasn't there they only had the SkyPark to bet on. After that, this was a very big building in the dark.

'Alison, baby? It's Mummy.'

The apartment lay mausoleum-silent before them.

Owen saw Wendy's shoulders fall with disappointment. He followed her as she made for Alison's bedroom and threw open the door in there. He played the flashlight across the room, lighting up posters of cartoon characters and some girl band that he didn't know. They had long legs, though. There were stuffed toys everywhere, but no sign of Alison.

Wendy went to the air vent and checked it, thinking that perhaps Alison had been there and gone again. But the cover was shut tightly. She sat heavily on the bed and grabbed one of the cuddly toys that lay on it. He watched as she buried her face in its fur and breathed the smell of her daughter that remained on it, and cried. Owen left her to her moment of pain. They needed to be moving on, but she would only slow him down until she recovered. He looked at the soft toys that were everywhere in the room. Some of them had been in movies when he'd been a kid. He picked one up and studied it nostalgically. None of them looked as well used as the pixie doll he'd seen her with.

'Looks like Mr Pickle is her favourite,' he said, for no particular reason.

Wendy nodded, and started to get her emotions under control again. She wiped her eyes with the heels of her palms. 'She takes him everywhere.'

'He looks kind of well-used,' he said. 'Funny how you can buy kids all these toys and they still stick with a battered old teddy with one eye, or something.'

'Do you have children?' Wendy asked him.

Owen shook his head and put the soft toy down. 'No.'

'Well, maybe one day.'

Owen said nothing, but she saw the muscles tighten in

his jaw and she knew that she had stumbled into badlands. Quickly, she said, 'That bloody Mr Pickle, he's probably crawling with germs.'

'He looks like he's been around a bit. Was he yours?'

'Mine? God no. He turned up at the hospital after she came out of intensive care. They had a toybox or something there on the children's ward. She must have got him out of that. When it was time to go home she wouldn't leave him behind.

'I suppose she thinks he helped her get better. Who knows, maybe he did?'

She got up off the bed and moved through into the lounge. Owen followed a moment later, and found her frozen to the spot, her eyes on the ceiling above her. He didn't need to throw the torchlight on it – he could already see the strange lights glowing within its bulging, rippling mass.

Owen's eyes measured the distance to the open apartment door, and wondered if he could tell Wendy to run for it. If she made it, why wouldn't the thing just go after her anyway? Whatever this was, nothing impeded it – it blew straight through molecular structures like a hurricane. There was no escape.

There was only one thing he could do.

'Wendy, get down!'

And even as he yelled, he was throwing himself at her – as the thing on the ceiling lurched downwards.

Instinctively, Wendy curled into a foetal ball, and Owen wrapped himself around her, covering her smaller body with his own, as he felt the slimy wetness of the thing that had come through the ceiling covering him.

Not only covering him, *probing him*. He could feel it inside him, seeping through his flesh, exploring his body, caressing his organs as if with cold, slimy fingers. He could feel it *tasting* him, and he felt a wave of nausea pass through him. He had felt this before, he remembered, the sensation of molecular invasion that had savaged his body and thrown him into unconsciousness.

Desperate, he fought off the darkness that threatened to sweep through his mind. He couldn't black out now. Because this time he knew it was different – it wasn't after him; it knew he was no good to it. It was trying to get through him, to pass through his body the way it passed through brick and steel to get to the woman beneath him. The only barrier that was stopping it was Owen's dead flesh and maybe – just maybe – his cellular corruption would poison it before it got to her.

He cried out with disgust and with a pain he had thought he would never feel again as the thing filled him, and his brain screamed for release, pleaded for the darkness that would save his sanity.

And Owen felt it in his head, felt its tentacles wrapping around the cells of his brain, squeezing them, bursting them.

And he thought he heard its voice.

Mummy!

Then it was gone.

Owen felt it leave his body like a sudden cold shudder.

Somebody just walked over my grave.

Yeah, he thought, *you wish!*

It was gone.

But he lay there a moment, conscious of Wendy beneath him, still curled into a ball, still breathing, and still there.

He rolled off her, his eyes searching the gloom for those strange lights. But there were none.

'What – what happened?' asked Wendy, her brain struggling for the moment to accept that she was still alive. 'Why didn't it kill us?'

Owen got to his feet and offered her his good hand. 'Sometimes it's better not to ask too many questions.'

He helped Wendy to her feet and told her that they had to go, wondering how the hell he was going to do what he knew lay ahead.

They left the apartment.

Lucca saw them go.

TWENTY-SIX

One day, when he'd had time on his hands, Jack had tried to work out how many times he had died. He actually sat down in his office with a block of paper and a couple of pens and wrote a neat *1* in the margin and alongside it he wrote *Dalek*.

That had been how it all started. After that there had been endless bar-room brawls – they had even killed him at Torchwood back in the early days – and at one time he'd worked in a travelling show billed as *The Man Who Cannot Die*. OK, people had paid to kill him then, but he figured that even if it bought him a few beers at the end of the day, when you got down to it a death was a death.

Then Torchwood had discovered that they had a problem with alien sleeper agents and the whole city started going up in smoke, and Jack lost the list and never got around to starting it again. The score was somewhere around a couple of hundred, by then. But he hadn't even started on the trenches in Flanders.

He was sure he had already forgotten some of them – unlike his lovers; he remembered all of *them* (every sex and species) – the one thing he never forgot, however, was how it felt to come back to life.

Like being dragged over broken glass.

It never got any better, and he never got used to it. It felt as bad as ever as he found himself lying on the concrete floor of the stairwell just outside the SkyPark.

Gwen was kneeling over him. She had seen him die so many times, but she never got used to it. A part of her never fully expected him to return to life.

This time, they had reached the twenty-fourth floor, had got through the stairway doors and had found themselves facing another door. Gwen had told him that, according to the plans on her hand-held module, this was an indoor sky-rise park area.

Jack had smiled. 'What a lovely day for a walk in the park.'

He had gone to push the door open and as soon as he had touched it, he'd been hit by enough volts to light up Cardiff Arms Park.

'I thought there was supposed to be a power cut around here,' he said as the feeling returned to his extremities and Gwen helped him up again.

'The door's electrified,' she said.

'No kidding?'

Jack was waving his hands in the air; his fingers still tingled from their contact with the door.

'Another of Lucca's defences.'

'Looks like.'

'So what do we do? With the lifts not working, there's no other way in.'

Jack was flexing his muscles, limbering up like a runner. 'We don't need another way in,' he said.

Gwen couldn't believe what he was suggesting. 'Jack that's madness.'

'Hey, immortality is all about getting a buzz out of life.'

'Jack—'

'Just get though fast and don't touch me. OK? Oh, and don't look. I might turn a bit… crispy. And you might try and hold your breath.'

Before Gwen could waste any more time arguing, Jack lunged at the door, throwing it open with the weight and momentum of his body even as the electricity hit him and surged through him.

Gwen leaped through the open doorway and then turned back, watching in horror as Jack – already dead – clung to the door, his flesh starting to cook, his eyes boiling in his head.

It didn't matter that she knew he was going to be all right…

She turned away, biting down on her hand. It was the only way to stop the scream that was clawing at her throat.

Behind her, she heard his body fall to the floor and the door swing to behind him. She found that she couldn't turn around. She couldn't bear to look at him like that.

She had seen him die so many times… but never like that.

She lost track of how long she stood there, her back to his body, waiting for him to stir.

When he touched her shoulder, she jumped.

'I told you not to look,' he said with a smile, and that old twinkle in his eyes.

His eyes. Thank God, he had eyes.

He saw her staring, wordless, and Jack felt a coldness close around his heart.

He ran a finger down the side of his face. 'Hey, everything *is* all right, isn't it?'

Gwen nodded smiling. 'Oh, yes. Perfect.'

All the same, Jack took his torch and checked his reflection carefully in one of the big SkyPark windows.

'Don't do that to me,' he said.

Together, they moved across the park as Gwen consulted the schematics on her small computer screen. They were looking at the outside of SkyPoint again, and Jack was running his eyes over the windows. He didn't want to choose the wrong one.

'Jack, are you sure this is going to work?'

He pointed at the electrified door. 'There's only one other way out of here, Gwen, and I am done cooking for today.'

There was a lightning conductor that ran down from the bottom end of Besnik Lucca's roof garden. Jack's plan was to climb it into the garden and launch a one-man assault on the penthouse from there. That in itself, at over sixty metres in the air, was a risky plan. Additionally, to get to the conductor, Jack would have to go out through one of the windows on the twenty-fourth floor and traverse half the SkyPoint building to reach it using a ledge only fifteen centimetres wide.

He was fairly confident that, however unassailable Lucca

considered his sanctuary, he wouldn't see an attack coming from the bottom of his garden.

'Don't worry,' he told Gwen. 'I'm good with heights.'

Then he drew the Webley, took careful aim and put out the window with four shots. The glass shattered and fell into the night. Jack hoped no one was standing down there tonight – that was the second window that he'd put out.

The wind whipped at his coat as he took a look out through the window and reloaded the gun. Gwen watched him fill the cylinder. Six shells. Then he pushed the Webley back into its holster and slipped the air force greatcoat off and handed it to Gwen.

'Keep this for me, will you? Batman looks great with that flapping cloak of his, but I don't think he ever gets this close to the edge.'

He stepped up onto the ledge and got ready to head along it.

'Which way is it, again?' he joked.

It was the final straw for Gwen, who threw the coat down on the floor and got up alongside him at the window.

'And where do you think you're going?' he asked.

'If you think you can take out Lucca and his men with just six bullets, you're crazy, Jack Harkness,' she said, and looked out at the drop below. 'Crazier than you think you are!'

'Oh no,' he said. 'You're crazy if you think you're coming out here with me.'

'I've been on ledges before. I talked a suicide down once, I did.'

'Oh, really? What storey?'

She hesitated. 'It's the principle of the thing that's important. Now let's move, I'm freezing my bloody knickers off here.'

TWENTY-SEVEN

The party was on the nineteenth floor. Owen and Wendy heard it as they went up the steps, echoing down the empty green-lit corridor.

Loud enough to wake the dead.

Chance would be a fine thing!

'We should take a look,' said Wendy.

Owen wasn't convinced. He had a pretty good idea of what was ahead of him now, and he wanted to get it done.

'If we've heard it, then maybe Alison has heard it. She might be there. That's got to be Alun and Julie. Alison likes them.'

Alun and Julie were the photographer and his girlfriend. He wasn't sure that Wendy was encouraging the right choice of friends for her daughter, but their options were limited at SkyPoint.

He thought of Alison reading Rapunzel to Mr Pickle.

Owen didn't want to use the last of their cleaning-product charges to get through the door – he was worried about his chances of survival in one piece a second time around, especially if he was blown down a couple of floors of concrete steps. Instead, he took the cover off the door locking mechanism with the point of Marion's carving knife and set about fusing the system. He wasn't Toshiko when it came to electronics, but you picked things up around Torchwood and there was still current running from some auxiliary source through the door locks, so it didn't take him long to get it open.

They followed the music, it was Evanescence. Not exactly party music, but each to his own.

Wendy was right. It took them to Alun and Julie's door. They had to hammer hard for a long time before they got an answer.

Alun came to the door in just his underpants.

'Don't tell me – you're complaining about the noise,' he said.

'Didn't you hear the alarm?' Owen asked.

'Alarm? What alarm? You're joking, right?'

His pupils were dilated like black holes. Alun was high. It didn't take much force to get past him, and Owen pushed his way into the flat.

Wendy followed. 'We're looking for Alison. You haven't seen her, have you?'

The apartment was lit by so many candles it made Owen think of a church. Or a black mass. Amy Lee was pouring out of a battery-powered boombox, singing about her Immortal. Julie with the Melons was lying semi-naked on the couch with a tourniquet around her arm and the hypodermic she had just injected still clutched in her hand.

'Oh, hi,' she said, trying to find the right muscles to make a smile with. 'Are we going to party?'

Owen turned off the music and looked at Wendy. 'You'd better hope Alison isn't here.'

Wendy looked horrified. Alun and Julie couldn't find any expressions at all.

'Stay there,' he said to her and tore the used hypodermic from Julie's hand. He wasn't sure if she even noticed.

'What are you doing?' Wendy shouted after him as Owen headed for the bathroom.

'I told you, stay there!'

Owen slammed the door shut after him.

Wendy felt scared and unsure. What was he doing in there? Why had he taken the hypodermic? Oh, God, she had put her daughter's safety in the hands of a junkie like Julie and Alun!

She hammered on the bathroom door for him to come out – she wanted to know what he was doing!

But Owen never got to tell her, because that was when the apartment door flew open and the knuckle-draggers finally showed up.

TWENTY-EIGHT

Fifteen centimetres, Jack had always insisted, was not nearly enough, not even when it had been six inches. He had, however, found on numerous occasions that you could work with what you were given.

Right now, it was all that was keeping him from falling over sixty metres to what, for him, would still be a pretty messy and uncomfortable resurrection. For Gwen, who moved slowly alongside him on the slender concrete ledge that skirted the circumference of SkyPoint, it would be certain death.

They had come maybe six metres, and it had taken them the best part of fifteen minutes. At this rate, they were going to reach Lucca in time to catch him eating breakfast on the terrace.

The night wind tore at his hair as he stood with his back to the SkyPoint wall, his arms spread, hands plastered against the concrete, feeling for the slightest grip. He could sense the toes of his boots sticking over the edge of the ledge and, immortal or not, it wasn't a comfortable place to be. He turned his head towards Gwen. She was half a metre away from him, stuck to the wall as he was by sheer will and the sweat of her palms.

'You doing OK?' he asked.

'Oh, yeah. Brilliant. You can see my house from here.'

Jack smiled, and moved his left foot a little further along the ledge, edging his shoulder along as he did so, then gently brought his right foot after him, keeping his centre of gravity as close to the wall behind him as possible. Then he watched as Gwen repeated the same action.

He tried to bring to mind the schematics of the building, tried to remember just how far they had said it was from the SkyPark window to the lightning conductor.

Twenty-four metres?

They weren't even halfway yet, and moving so slowly had never seemed so exhausting.

Distantly, he heard the sounds of cars in the city below. Night owls heading home, and shift workers making for the plant. He had travelled to a lot of worlds in his time, but that one seemed stranger than most, and so much more than just sixty metres away. A world of mortgage repayments, office jobs, pension plans and family. Not his world, and never would be.

He moved along the ledge a little more.

At least the air was good up here. It was coming straight in off the Bristol Channel and, beyond that, the Atlantic. There was no air on any planet quite as good as the air that came in off the Atlantic.

'You keeping up?' he called to Gwen.

He saw her nod. But she didn't look at him now, she was keeping her eyes dead ahead. Concentrating. Feeling her way along the side of the building. Shifting sideways, moving one foot slowly along after the other.

Jack worried about her, but there was nothing he could do now. She had been determined to join him, and arguing with her would just have used up more time. Besides, she was right, six shells wasn't a lot to take out a man like Lucca and however many heavies he might have shoring up his fortress defences. In his experience, guns were like heads, two were always better than one. Unless they were pointing your way, of course.

He continued to move along the ledge and found he was getting into a rhythm now; everything starting to fit into a pattern, his movement and his breathing – even the gusts of Atlantic air were coming at the right time. He felt that he was moving faster.

Then he saw the gulls.

There were six of them – big, grey-backed herring gulls – roosting on the ledge. As Jack inched ever closer, the first bird turned and looked at him, then looked away as if it thought it was seeing things, or maybe that the humans would fall off before they got much closer. Either way, the bird didn't move.

'Looks like we got company up here,' Jack said to Gwen.

'What?' she demanded, as in, *what the hell are you talking about?*

'You don't have any mackerel or anything on you, do you?'

'Jack, what is going on?'

From her position, she couldn't see the gulls. Jack decided it wouldn't be a problem, the birds would move. After all, people were bigger than birds, right?

But as Jack drew closer, the birds didn't move. The closest one looked over at him again and stretched, beat its wings, and cried out into the night. That set off its companions, who took up the chorus. But they didn't take off, as he'd expected.

'Come on, guys, move along,' Jack said, as he got within half a metre of the gulls.

Instead, the first gull edged towards him and stabbed at his boot with its beak.

'Hey! You little freak!'

Jack kicked out at the bird and it hopped back in retreat, but as Jack took his next step the bird darted forward again and attacked his boot.

Jack lashed out with his foot. 'Get out of it!'

And this time, the bird leaped into the night, and took its friends with it. Suddenly the air around Jack and Gwen was filled with the thunder of beating wings and crying gulls.

'Oh my God, Jack!'

Jack reached out and grabbed Gwen's hand.

'Just stay calm,' he said.

Right now the birds were just showboating, making a lot of noise, warning off the invaders to their territory, maybe still a little intimidated by their size. But these weren't sparrows, and if they decided to swing in for an attack they were in trouble. Gulls had big, sharp beaks, and they were also the only ones up here that could fly.

It didn't take much working out.

'Hey, you lot, shut up!'

The voice came from above them. It was a thin voice, like it had come out of some sort of woodwind instrument played badly.

'Noisy buggers, piss off!'

This second voice was deeper, more brass section.

Two men right above them in Besnik Lucca's garden had been attracted by the commotion of the gulls. Jack and Gwen stopped breathing.

'Here, now get off!'

It was Brass again, and as he spoke Jack saw a chunk of what looked like burger roll fly over the side of the building. As one, the gulls dived after it into the night below.

Jack felt himself take another breath.

Above him Woodwind was telling Brass how he hated those bloody things; one had swept down on him in Tenby when he was a kid and stolen his ice cream right out of his hand.

Maybe that was where his life had all gone wrong, thought Jack. An incident like that was going to screw a kid up – ice cream robbery: it was the kind of thing that would make a sociopath out of anybody.

He heard the voices of Lucca's two men move away, and glanced back at Gwen. She looked exhausted, but he knew she was tough. She would make it.

Fifteen minutes later, Jack found the lightning conductor.

Turning around to climb up the conductor was always going to be tricky, and he had been rehearsing the move in his head as he edged towards it. With his back to the wall, he wrapped the fingers of his left hand around the rod and used them to brace himself as he reached over his shoulder with his other hand. With a little quick footwork he found himself facing the right way round and hauled himself nimbly up the wall, knowing that Gwen would work out the move for herself and follow him up.

After the age it had taken them to edge around the outside of SkyPoint, Jack found himself rolling over the balcony wall into Lucca's verdant roof garden only ten seconds later. He dropped to the floor in a crouch and Gwen was beside him a moment later.

Jack drew the Webley from its holster.

TWENTY-NINE

The goons that had burst into the photographer's flat – the men that Jack would soon after think of as Woodwind and Brass – had left Alun and Julie behind. The young couple were stoned out of their heads and probably wouldn't remember the visit if they survived the night. The only people that the thugs were interested in were Wendy and Owen, and Owen didn't put up a fight.

When he heard them crash through the apartment door, he had finished what he had gone to do in the bathroom, and stepped out.

His only words were to Wendy: 'Just do as they say.'

There was no real option for them. The men weren't waving guns around, but they didn't need to. Even a living, breathing Owen whose bones would fix wouldn't have been much of a match for Lucca's slabs of muscle.

Woodwind and Brass shoved Owen and Wendy out of the flat, and ushered them towards the steps. Before they reached them, Owen heard Evanescence pouring out of the flat once again.

Owen and Wendy were taken up to the twenty-first floor and led along the corridor to what looked like a broom cupboard. It proved to be a secret lift hidden behind a panel. Thirty seconds later, he and Wendy were led into Lucca's apartment. Woodwind and Brass left them there.

Owen saw Toshiko, still secured to the chair, and went to her, filled with a mix of relief and rage.

'Tosh, are you all right?'

'I'm fine, Owen. I'm sorry, I messed up, didn't I?'

'No, course you didn't,' he said.

Lucca stood watching, amused.

'You two make such a beautiful couple,' he said. 'You should really get together.'

'Screw you, Lucca,' Owen snarled. 'What do you want?'

Lucca spread his arms, took in the apartment. 'Look about you, Owen. I am a successful man.'

Owen took in the money that hung on the walls at a glance. 'You're a bloody crook.'

Neither Lucca's smile nor his pride faltered. 'I have many interests. I am a man of culture. Success brings with it the opportunity to better oneself, to learn. To study.'

'What are you, an advert for the Open University?'

Lucca was patient. 'When this mysterious thing started to take people here at SkyPoint the average man's reaction would have been fear, would have been to run. But I am very far from average.'

'Yeah, well you would say that, wouldn't you?' Owen taunted.

'My reaction, Owen, was to study, and learn.'

Lucca had taken the TV remote in his other hand, and he aimed it at the big set. On screen, Owen saw Gwen and Rhys being led into the show apartment by a man he guessed to be Brian Shaw. The camera cut to a new location – a bathroom: as Brian Shaw walked in and was consumed by the amorphous thing that came out of the wall. He felt Wendy stiffen next to him as she watched. The scene switched to another room and someone that Owen didn't recognise being swallowed by the thing. In another room, another victim…

'You recorded all of this?' Owen gasped.

'I have cameras everywhere. I see everything.'

'And exactly what have you learned?' asked Toshiko.

'How sick you are?' suggested Owen.

Sticks and stones didn't even leave a mark on Besnik Lucca. He played something else on the television. It was the Lloyds' apartment an hour ago. Owen covering Wendy with his body, saving her from the mass of rippling, glowing matter that enveloped them.

'The man who sees everything, knows everything,' said Lucca, and he took a couple of steps towards Owen. 'Now I want to know about you.'

Owen felt Lucca's eyes boring into him. 'Yeah, well I like to preserve an air of mystery. Makes me more attractive to women.'

Lucca put the gun against Owen's temple. 'How about if I put a hole in your head. How attractive do you think that will make you?'

'Leave him alone!'

Lucca swung around as Toshiko cried out. He slipped

behind the steel chair and pressed the gun against her neck. Owen saw her eyes swell with fear.

'Get away from her,' Owen said.

'Then tell me what you are,' Lucca said. 'Why did it refuse you? Twice?'

Owen looked from him to Toshiko and shrugged. 'Because I'm dead.'

'Don't you play with me!'

Owen could see his finger tightening on the trigger.

'It's true!' And Owen ripped apart his shirt, revealing the bullet hole. 'I got shot through the heart. But I'm still alive. That's why the thing – whatever it is – won't take me, it needs living cellular matter to survive. And I'm not alive.'

He glanced towards Wendy. She looked like she was going to be sick.

Lucca stared at Owen. 'You're undead.'

'I don't sleep in a coffin or anything. In fact, I don't sleep.'

Lucca was closing on him again, walking around him. 'Fascinating. Fascinating. The living dead. Tell me, do you feel pain?'

'Not pain, as such.'

Lucca kicked him in the shin.

'All the same, I'd rather you didn't do that.'

Lucca laughed, a great booming laugh. Like he'd heard the funniest joke in the world. Like he was mad.

Suddenly he pushed the gun up under Owen's head. 'If I blow your head off, will you run around like something off a cartoon?'

Owen could see Toshiko. She was crying.

And he thought maybe Lucca would do it. Maybe he would pull the trigger and end this cruel, sick joke his life had turned into.

But the last thing he would see, the thing he would take into the darkness with him, would be Toshiko crying.

Behind his back, Owen pulled Ewan's phone from his pocket. He knew where the call button was. He pushed it.

And Lucca's phone started to ring.

Lucca glanced away – just for a second.

Owen brought his knee up hard into Lucca's crotch. As Lucca doubled over, Owen kicked the gun from his hand, and went for him again – but Lucca came up with the switchblade in his hand, and lurched towards Toshiko.

'Maybe I can't kill you. But there are worse things than death.' He had the knife at Toshiko's throat.

'Maybe you'd like to put that to the test!'

It was Jack. He was standing just inside the garden doors, the Webley aimed straight at Lucca.

As Lucca turned to look at Jack, Gwen pressed her automatic behind his ear and took the knife out of his hand. She used to it cut Toshiko free.

'I have men. You'll never get out alive,' he said.

'You mean Mr Woodwind and Mr Brass?' said Jack. 'They went to feed the birds.'

Lucca smiled. 'You'll never get out alive,' he said again.

Gwen followed his eyes. He was looking across the apartment to where a little girl with golden hair stood. She looked sleepy, as if she had just woken up. She held a strange rag doll in her arms with candy-striped trousers and turned-up shoes.

'What's going on?' she said.

Wendy saw her. 'Alison!'

She lurched towards her, but Owen caught her wrist.

'No, don't go near her.'

Wendy looked at him, her eyes full of rage and confusion. 'What the hell do you mean?'

'Why are you aiming guns at Mr Lucca?' she asked. 'Mr Lucca is my friend.'

'It's OK, little girl,' said Jack. 'Just go back to your room. Everything is going to be fine.'

'Alison!' cried Wendy.

'It's all right, Mummy. But Mr Pickle says we have to help Mr Lucca. Mr Lucca is our friend.'

'Alison, Mr Lucca is a bad man. You shouldn't be friends with him,' said Gwen.

'But I understand you, don't I?' said Lucca, looking at the child. 'I know who you are, don't I?'

'She's my daughter!' Wendy shouted.

Owen said, 'He's not talking to Wendy. He's talking to Mr Pickle.'

Wendy snarled like an animal. 'What? You're mad! You're mad! Let me go!' She started to rain blows on Owen.

Toshiko went to him. Held Wendy. 'Please, Mrs Lloyd, be calm.'

Jack had moved in closer to Lucca now, still had him covered by the Webley. Alison stood in the middle of the room, holding Mr Pickle in her arms.

'OK, Owen,' Jack said calmly, keeping an eye on the girl as much as Lucca, 'do you want to tell me that Mr Pickle isn't the sad-looking pixie doll she's holding.'

Alison turned to look at him as Owen spoke. 'Mr Pickle is a thought-form. You know, like some yogis in the Himalayas are supposed to be able to create after years of concentration.'

'What?' said Gwen. 'They can just think a creature into existence?'

'Oh yes,' said Lucca. 'A servant to do their bidding. There are many stories.'

'Don't be ridiculous,' snapped Wendy. 'She's just a little girl.'

Owen addressed Jack and Gwen. 'Alison had a car crash. She died at the scene for five minutes. She brought something back with her. Something that in hospital became manifested by her as a doll, Mr Pickle.'

'But the thought-form couldn't maintain its physical form indefinitely without cellular matter,' Jack guessed.

He looked across at Lucca. 'And you worked all that out?'

'I saw it. And I made friends with Alison and Mr Pickle.'

'In the name of learning?' Owen asked, his voice dry with sarcasm.

'And survival,' he said. 'When Torchwood showed up, it sensed that it was under threat. That was why its attacks increased.'

Toshiko looked at the girl. If she understood any of this she gave no sign. The doll remained cradled in her arms, and looked like nothing but a doll.

'That is why,' Lucca said. 'You won't get out of this room alive. The thought-form knows who its friends are, and who are its enemies.'

And that was when Mr Pickle started to shimmer in Alison's arms. As they watched, the doll transformed into a cloud of rippling light and slime, and Alison fell to the floor, unconscious.

Wendy screamed and tried to run to her daughter, but Toshiko held her tight, and the thought-form swept across the room towards Toshiko.

Owen leaped between them.

'You want her? You're going to have to take a bit of me first!'

And from his pocket he drew the hypodermic that he had snatched from Julie in the flat. It was filled with a dark, almost black substance. Owen raised his fist and pushed home the needle. The black liquid sprayed across the inside of the thought-form, attaching itself to the strange sunburst lights within it.

As they watched the lights began to dim, and the thought-form began to writhe, sweeping this way and that, rippling and sagging.

And then it was gone.

Lucca stared around in horror. 'You killed it!'

Toshiko released Wendy, who rushed to her fallen child. 'Alison! Alison!'

Owen was at her side. 'Let me look at her.'

He felt for a pulse. There wasn't one.

'What's going on?' demanded Jack.

'Tosh,' Owen commanded. 'Quick, I need you to give her mouth to mouth.'

Then he started to give her heart massage, talking quickly as he worked. 'I worked out the thought-form needed living cellular matter. That was why it left me on the floor. I'm dead tissue, I was bad for it. So I pumped it full of my blood.

'Trouble is, the thought-form was linked to Alison. She brought it back with her. It's entangled with her being. Killing it could kill her.'

Toshiko was giving Alison the kiss of life.

Owen had his hands on her sternum, pressing, counting. And he found himself praying – if God didn't exist, then maybe something else might hear him. He didn't want her to go back into the dark again.

'You have to save her!' cried Wendy. 'Alison, come back to me darling, come back.'

'Come on, Alison. Come back. Out of the dark, darling. Out of the dark.'

And then Owen was aware of something beneath his hands.

Her heart?

'Quick, Tosh,' he said. 'Check her pulse!'

And then Alison coughed, and her eyes opened.

Alison wrapped her arms around her mother and hugged her tighter than anything in her life.

Owen looked at Toshiko, and they smiled.

Owen thought it felt good to smile.

THIRTY

Ianto was waiting for them outside SkyPoint with the SUV when they came out of reception with Besnik Lucca, his hands fixed behind him with cable-ties. They left him sitting on the steps of the central police station with his ankles also bound with plastic and a package slung around his neck. Gwen made a call as the SUV screeched away and when the cops opened what hung around Lucca's neck they found all the digital detail they needed to put him away for half a century.

They took the SUV back to Roald Dahl Plass, but Owen didn't go with the others down to the Hub. He said he'd been cooped up in that bloody skyscraper too long, and he needed some air.

It was half past four in the morning. It wouldn't be long before dawn broke. There might be time for just one coffee down at Constantine's before the sun came up.

When he got there the café was empty.

This was no-man's-hour for the nightshift workers and

the clubbers. Neither the night before, nor the day after. In another hour or so there would be the early-shift workers, but until then nobody. Owen wondered if it was even worth buying the cup of coffee that he wouldn't drink.

The chances of the twins showing up now were pretty remote.

What the hell? Where else are you going to go?

He walked down to the counter, but the kid wasn't there. Owen thought he'd probably gone to the bathroom, or was maybe taking a drag out back.

Then he heard something break.

There was a doorway behind the bar. Owen had no idea where it led – some sort of kitchen, he had always assumed. It sounded like a bottle breaking. A milk bottle. Nothing too strange about that in a coffee shop, he thought. Only afterwards there was no curse, no sound of someone sweeping it up.

Owen's senses were electrified. He moved around the counter and into the kitchen area behind it.

The coffee shop kid – or what was left of him – was on the floor. The twins had divided him between them again and were quickly and efficiently devouring him.

Owen felt sorry for the kid. And that it was maybe his fault that he was dead.

Owen stepped into their line of vision and the two sisters looked up at him, with their shark eyes, blood and tatters of meat hanging from their distended savage jaws.

'Ladies,' he said.

This was a moment he had thought about a great deal since that first night hiding behind the rubbish while the girls chewed up the ponytailed French student. If ever there was a more certain way of ending this walking death, he couldn't think what it could be. To be torn apart, eaten and digested by two carnivorous predators might be painful – but couldn't be any worse than what he had been enduring. And he had seen that they were quick. More importantly, he couldn't believe that there was any chance that his consciousness would survive. If he gave himself to them, it would be over.

No doubt.

They looked at him and he could see that they were hungry for more.

'Come and get it,' he said.

They looked at each other, and he could have sworn they actually smiled. And then they pounced.

And Owen pulled the automatic from inside his coat and tore them to pieces in mid-air with a spray of bullets.

He stepped back as the dead meat hit the kitchen floor tiles with a wet slap next to what had been their last supper.

He slid his gun back inside his jacket and checked himself in a grease-spotted mirror by the doorway for any blood-spray. He looked fine. For a dead man.

Quickly, he slipped back around the counter and got out of the coffee shop. The last thing he needed was to meet any customers coming in.

Instead he ran into Toshiko. She was waiting for him outside the door.

'Tosh?'

'I'm sorry. I needed a walk, too.'

'You mean you followed me?' he said.

She didn't try to lie, there was no point. 'What were you doing in there? You don't drink coffee. You can't.'

Owen pulled up his coat collar, the first threads of morning were starting to show in the sky and he thought the first chill of the autumn was coming with it.

'You know, that's right,' he smiled. 'But do you know something else, there's so much more to life.'

She smiled, and wanted to take his hand. But didn't.

They walked a few steps along the road in silence. A rubbish truck rumbled past them as Cardiff started to come to life.

When he turned to her again, he wasn't smiling any more.

'I don't want to go back into the dark, Tosh,' he said. 'Not ever.'

ACKNOWLEDGEMENTS

A writer's greatest friend should always be his editor. A good one can make you seem so much better than you really are – so my greatest thanks to Steve Tribe for, if nothing else, the patience of a saint. Also to Gary Russell for his encouragement, talent and hard work in all we have done together.

Thanks also to Hayley for putting up with a clattering keyboard into the the wee hours, and to all the cast of *Torchwood* – particularly Burn and Naoko, who brought Owen and Toshiko to life and then so beautifully took them into death. I will miss you!

But biggest thanks to Russell for creating such marvellous shows and proving that there is a place for fantasy on British TV, and thanks also – and to Julie – for letting me be a part of it.

Also available from BBC Books

TORCHWOOD
THE TWILIGHT STREETS
Gary Russell

ISBN 978 1 846 07439 4
UK £6.99 US$11.99/$14.99 CDN

There's a part of the city that no one much goes to, a collection of rundown old houses and gloomy streets. No one stays there long, and no one can explain why – something's not quite right there.

Now the Council is renovating the district, and a new company is overseeing the work. There will be street parties and events to show off the newly gentrified neighbourhood: clowns and face-painters for the kids, magicians for the adults – the street entertainers of Cardiff, out in force.

None of this is Torchwood's problem. Until Toshiko recognises the sponsor of the street parties: Bilis Manger.

Now there is something for Torchwood to investigate. But Captain Jack Harkness has never been able to get into the area; it makes him physically ill to go near it. Without Jack's help, Torchwood must face the darker side of urban Cardiff alone...

Featuring Captain Jack Harkness as played by John Barrowman, with Gwen Cooper, Owen Harper, Toshiko Sato and Ianto Jones as played by Eve Myles, Burn Gorman, Naoki Mori and Gareth David-Lloyd, in the hit series created by Russell T Davies for BBC Television.

Also available from BBC Books

TORCHWOOD

PACK ANIMALS

Peter Anghelides

ISBN 978 1 846 07574 2
UK £6.99 US$11.99/$14.99 CDN

Shopping for wedding gifts is enjoyable, unless like Gwen you witness a Weevil massacre in the shopping centre. A trip to the zoo is a great day out, until a date goes tragically wrong and Ianto is badly injured by stolen alien tech. And Halloween is a day of fun and frights, before unspeakable monsters invade the streets of Cardiff and it's no longer a trick or a treat for the terrified population.

Torchwood can control small groups of scavengers, but now someone has given large numbers of predators a season ticket to Earth. Jack's investigation is hampered when he finds he's being investigated himself. Owen is convinced that it's just one guy who's toying with them. But will Torchwood find out before it's too late that the game is horribly real, and the deck is stacked against them?

Featuring Captain Jack Harkness as played by John Barrowman, with Gwen Cooper, Owen Harper, Toshiko Sato and Ianto Jones as played by Eve Myles, Burn Gorman, Naoki Mori and Gareth David-Lloyd, in the hit series created by Russell T Davies for BBC Television.

Also available from BBC Books

TORCHWOOD
ALMOST PERFECT
James Goss

ISBN 978 1 846 07573 5
UK £6.99 US$11.99/$14.99 CDN

Emma is 30, single and frankly desperate. She woke up this morning with nothing to look forward to but another evening of unsuccessful speed-dating. But now she has a new weapon in her quest for Mr Right. And it's made her almost perfect.

Gwen Cooper woke up this morning expecting the unexpected. As usual. She went to work and found a skeleton at a table for two and a colleague in a surprisingly glamorous dress. Perfect.

Ianto Jones woke up this morning with no memory of last night. He went to work, where he caused amusement, suspicion and a little bit of jealousy. Because Ianto Jones woke up this morning in the body of a woman. And he's looking just about perfect.

Jack Harkness has always had his doubts about Perfection.

Featuring Captain Jack Harkness as played by John Barrowman, with Gwen Cooper and Ianto Jones as played by Eve Myles and Gareth David-Lloyd, in the hit series created by Russell T Davies for BBC Television.

Also available from BBC Books

THE TORCHWOOD ARCHIVES

ISBN 978 1 846 07459 2
£14.99

Separate from the Government
Outside the police
Beyond the United Nations…

Founded by Queen Victoria in 1879, the Torchwood Institute has long battled against alien threats to the British Empire. The Torchwood Archives is an insider's look into the secret world of this unique investigative team.

In-depth background on personnel, case files on alien enemies of the Crown and descriptions of extra-terrestrial technology collected over the years will uncover more about the world of Torchwood than ever previously known, including some of the biggest mysteries surrounding the Rift in space and time running through Cardiff.

Based on the hit series
created by Russell T Davies
for BBC Television.